YOUR COWBOY IS GONE

YOUR COWBOY IS GONE

A Novel

Ron McCoy

MANY**SEASONS**PRESS

Mesa, Arizona • 2023

FIRST EDITION

Your Cowboy is Gone
A Novel

Copyright © 2023 Ron McCoy

MANY**SEASONS**PRESS

Published by Many Seasons Press
an Imprint of Multimedia Publishing Project
PO Box 50553
Mesa, Arizona 85208-0028
480-939-9689 | MultimediaPublishingProject.com

Book designed by Yolie Hernandez
(AZBookDesigner@icloud.com)

Paperback ISBN: 978-1-956203-25-7

Library of Congress Control Number: 2023934897

Printed in the United States of America.

CONTENTS

CONTENTS

ACKNOWLEDGEMENTS

It's great to have people spur you on when writing. A great deal of comments, encouragement, and motivation come from people who read *"Campfire Tales"* and *"Murder at the Joshua Tree."* Many of whom I don't really know, but the comments come from book signings and I really appreciate it.

Cathie Ringering and John Nudge read *"Your Cowboy is Gone"* and did an incredible job with their comments and suggestions. Members of the Apache Junction Writers Club have always been supporting and encouraging. My publisher, Many Seasons Press, rounds this fabulous group off with her talent and expertise.

You have all been my inspiration and encouragement to keep on going with my writings.

Last of all, a heartfelt thanks to the many wonderful people I have met at my book signings. You make this fun and worthwhile.

1

SALLY ARRIVES IN NEBRASKA

The ancient Union Pacific locomotive clanked and wheezed into the Riverton, Nebraska, railroad station. It was the end of the line for this run and the beginning of the return run to Omaha.

The engineer began to tank up the locomotive's water reservoir with four thousand five hundred gallons of water for the return run. The express car attached to the coal tender, doors were thrown open, exposing the express agent and station agent to the cold, snowy January weather that came with no hope of improvement. The cold wind blunted their conversation. The express agent began stacking mail, freight, and packages by the express car door. Then the station agent loaded all of this onto his express cart.

It turned out that the passenger car had only one traveler, and she would be getting off in Riverton. As they spoke of this, a young woman disembarked from the passenger car and headed their way. She didn't appear to be too tall and was slightly built. She wore a thin, worn coat and a mid-calf length dress. Worn old shoes were on her feet, and her uncovered light brown hair was collecting snowflakes, drawing attention to her obviously stressed facial expression. Pale, tired, and worn out, she asked which door led to the waiting room.

"This way, Miss," the station agent answered. "Not that it's much warmer inside. They are phasing out the old steam engines. When the new diesel engines come on the line, Union Pacific will phase out this station and use a new one over in Middletown. We are still here because this is the only place available that can supply four thousand five hundred to ten thousand gallons of water for these steam engines. So, it doesn't seem practical to do much in the way of repair work on this old station. I know it was here in 1906. That was some forty years ago. Oh my! How time slips by."

She entered the waiting room and sat down while he rushed outside for his now loaded express cart.

The train pulled forward and proceeded to a spur line. There, the brakeman threw the switch, and the train backed onto the main line. Again, the switch was thrown by the brakeman, who jumped into the caboose as it passed. The engineer then jerked the throttle open and roared past the tiny station.

It all settled down and became quiet. Only the wind was heard as it rattled the loose boards on the station siding. The station agent approached the woman after sorting the deliveries.

"You have someone coming to pick you up?" he asked.

With sad eyes, she said, "No, but I'll wait for the next train going west to Wyoming."

With that, he said, "There won't be another train going west for three days." He added that there were no overnight accommodations in Riverton or restaurants for that matter. Then he asked, "What does your ticket show for the connecting train?"

She looked at him hesitantly and said, "I don't have a ticket. I had bought one in Cleveland for Chicago, hoping my fiancé would send money for the next part of my trip, but he didn't. So, I bought a ticket to Omaha with all the money I had left. The conductor in Omaha saw that my ticket didn't allow continued passage but allowed me to ride here to Riverton as there wasn't anybody else in the passenger car. Anyway, I'm here now, totally broke, and can only hope my fiancé will send some money, but how or to where I don't know."

"Well, Miss," the agent said, "My name is Carl, and I have no idea how to help you. I am required to lock up the station at five p.m."

"Carl, my name is Sally Wilson, and I can just wait outside until morning."

"No, you can't. You'll freeze to death the way you're dressed. I'll leave enough coal for the heater to keep it going, and here is an old army blanket. Be sparing with the coal since it's all I've got. I'll lock up, but you can leave the building if you need to. Just lock up when you come back. It's predicted to be below zero tomorrow, and this is the best that I can do."

As she threw the blanket over her shoulders, Carl noticed she was in the family way.

January 1947 was certainly bringing in new challenges, Carl thought.

2

MEETING PATSY

Night soon fell in the lonely, cold waiting room. A single light bulb hanging from the ceiling was the only light to ward off total darkness.

Sally, with much effort, pulled one of the waiting room benches over to the coal-fired furnace. After sitting there for a while, she decided to look around for something more comfortable to lie on or cover up with. All she found was an old quilt, and knowing that anything was better than nothing, she decided to use it to cover up with. She spread some old feed sacks on the bench to lie on. She fell asleep, awakening only to feed the furnace when she became cold.

Morning came. The wind blew all night, and the drafty, old station even allowed fine snow to blow in through the many cracks in the walls. The inside and outside walls needed repair and paint badly, but considering the Union Pacific plans to phase out the station fairly soon, this was impractical.

Sally had made it through the night by the coal-fired furnace, but she never really warmed up. She did feed the heater sparingly, but the waiting room was large, and with the cold blowing in so easily, it was almost impossible to warm up adequately.

Carl showed up right at nine a.m. and opened up the station. He had brought a peanut butter and jelly sandwich from home and offered it to Sally. She said, "No, thanks."

"Okay, I'll just throw it out."

"Well, in that case, I'll take it."

A steam locomotive pulled in the same setup and delivery of express goods. No passengers. This time Carl hit up the fireman on the locomotive for a couple of large buckets of coal.

At eleven a.m., the front door opened, and a well-dressed but casual, slender young woman with reddish brown hair came in with a "Hi Carl, anything for us in the last couple of days?"

"Anne, I got your packages stacked up on the freight cart." With that, they carried them out and put them into a Buick. They went inside for Anne to pay the freight bill. Anne noticed Sally sitting by the coal furnace. "What's with her?" she asked.

Carl explained what he knew briefly and added he didn't know what to do with her, not to mention that she was in the family way.

"Carl, introduce me, and I'll take her up to Patsy Monroe's place. We'll feed her, warm her up and maybe even find her lost fiancé."

Carl simply took her over to Sally and introduced them. "Sally Wilson, this is Anne. She'll take you to her home for a while."

The two women walked out to the still-running Buick with the heater running full blast. Anne related to Sally how she felt about the weather, the closing of the station, and just about anything that came to her mind. After passing through the town of Riverton and going down a country road, they came to a large, ornate three-story house with a turret at one end. It was well-kept and appeared to have been built in the 1880s. They hurried inside carrying the packages. Anne took Sally to a room on the ground floor of the turret to meet Patsy Monroe.

There they found Patsy finishing her breakfast. Patsy was of average height, had dyed red hair, and was somewhat overweight and heavily made up, making it difficult to guess her age. She jumped upon seeing Sally and gave her a big hug to welcome her. She began talking as if they had known each other forever.

Patsy called for Violet, her housekeeper and chief cook. "Bring our guest here whatever she wants to eat or drink. She looks like she missed breakfast today."

This opened up a conversation in which Sally unloaded all of her problems. She couldn't believe what she told them about her fiancé, Captain Tom Warfield, who was unexpectedly called away to a remote army post called Camp Wood in Wyoming.

He was an army engineer and had been needed right away. Tom had left so suddenly that she couldn't tell him she might be pregnant. When she was sure, she told her parents, who, in their outrage, immediately threw her out of the house. Her letters to Tom went unanswered. With money running out, she decided to go to Camp Wood. Now everything had fallen apart. She was filled with hopelessness. The cold weather and lack of food for the last ten days weren't doing her or her baby any good.

She broke down and cried uncontrollably. Patsy told Violet, "Let's get her a hot bath, clean her up with some fresh clothes and get her into bed. Use the second-floor room above mine."

3

JOB ON RANCH

Two days later, Sally appeared at the breakfast table, refreshed and well-rested. She was almost cheerful. Anne had helped her with her hair. Sally was greeted warmly by Patsy and three other young women at the table, where they were engaged in small talk. Anne introduced them as, Memory, who appeared to be energetic and the most outgoing of the group; Kat, a shorter blond with a quiet, reserved demeanor; and Hope, who was tall and willowy with dark blond hair.

Patsy interrupted all of this by saying, "Sally, I have something for you to consider that can help both of us out and earn you some money to continue your trip. There is an old rancher named Sweeny, who I look after. He lives about fifteen miles from here. We have some business interests together. He lives out on his ranch by himself. We realize we're all getting a bit older and more subject to accidents and illnesses. If something happened to him, I would never forgive myself. One of the girls drives out to the ranch once a week to check on him and bring groceries and whatever else he needs. He has some four hundred head of cattle, so he has more chores to do than he can get done in the time he has. So the housework just doesn't get done, and I suspect his meals are lacking too. We need someone out there to make sure he hasn't had an accident or gotten sick—also to cook and clean the house for him. We'll pay you a weekly wage, and there won't be any expense to you. I've talked to him, and he said some company would be great. I can have Anne drive you out there tomorrow, and you can size the job up better."

Sally now beamed with hope and expressed her deep gratitude.

The following morning came with newfound hope for Sally. She and Anne loaded up a four-wheel drive pickup equipped with chains, veterinarian supplies, motor oil, and various other items Sweeny had requested. They also brought much-needed grocery items for him.

"We'll need these chains and four-wheel drive once we get off the main road. Then we'll have about ten miles of little used ranch road, which the County doesn't snowplow," Anne commented.

They started out. The sun shone on the new fallen snow from yesterday. The frozen crystals sparkled in the sun's rays. Anne kept talking about the area and Ol' Man Sweeny, which sparked Sally's interest in this place.

Anne suddenly blurted out, "Our turn off is right here. Oh my gosh! Look! Somebody has snow plowed the road out, especially for us, maybe? There are only two people who live on this road. Sweeny is at the end, and Lester Bunch is about halfway up. It certainly wasn't Lester. He prefers that amber drink and rarely gets out."

Sally said, "Do you think Sweeny is trying to impress us?"

"Not us, you," Anne stated.

"How do you know that?" Sally cheerfully asked.

"I've never, and I mean never, seen this road plowed clear of snow before," Anne said.

They both laughed hard about this. Anne gained some composure and said, "At least it would appear that he really wants to further his cause in making such a good impression."

The plowed road ended up at the Sweeny ranch. They drove up to the front porch of a log house. The big porch was covered with a roof, and the snow was shoveled off the porch, as was the drive, the walk, and the porch steps.

Anne just looked at Sally and said, "This is quite a welcome!"

With that, the front door flew open, and there stood Ol' Man Sweeny. He was thin, with gray and thinning hair, and wearing cowboy boots. Clean, new-looking jeans and a plaid flannel shirt completed his attire. He was energetically pulling on an old Parka.

"Come on in and get out of the cold. I've got fresh coffee ready and some cinnamon rolls. Don't worry about the groceries. I'll get them once I get you both inside."

Sally could see several buildings, one of which was the main barn with some corrals, all of which seemed to be in good repair. While the girls were enjoying their hot coffee and rolls, Sweeny got everything inside and then gave them a house tour.

Sally was impressed with the spacious kitchen, abundant cabinet space, new and modern appliances, and a variety of kitchen gadgets. After the grand tour, they sat in the living room in front of a cozy fire in the fireplace. As they relaxed, Sally could size up Sweeny better. He looked to be in his mid-seventies, and his gray hair needed to be cut, but he was clean-shaven and had strong, calloused hands. She guessed he was about six feet tall with a twinkle in his eye. He certainly was the genuine cowboy that she expected.

Sweeny was not only a hard worker but educated as well, seeing the variety of books on the shelves by such authors as Tennessee Williams, John Steinbeck, Ernest Hemingway, and other notable authors. A few of the magazines on the coffee table, she also noted. She was no literary scholar herself, but with difficult parents, she frequently hid in her room and read books she had found at the library. Thus far, she was enjoying his company and found him very relaxed.

There seemed to be an abundance of firewood, but clearly no trees around. So Sally inquired, "Where do you find firewood around here? I don't see any trees."

Sweeny replied, "That's very observant of you. We do need to have a lot of firewood on hand. We also have lots of backup firewood in case the electricity goes out, which sometimes happens in the winter. We have a generator and a large propane tank out back. There is also a five-hundred-gallon gas tank down by the barn for the ranch truck and generator. As far as having enough wood in this treeless area, one weekend a year, the local good ol' boys drive over to a wooded area some seventy miles from here. We cut the dead trees and split the wood. We load it all into our trucks and trailers and divide it up between us. That's in case our other resources fail when and if the electricity goes out, which has happened," he said with a smile.

Sweeny had a part collie dog named Benny, and Sweeny claimed the black and white dog was his best friend.

"How so?" Anne queried.

"He doesn't ask for much and doesn't have anything to say or bother me with and pretty much keeps to himself."

With that and nails clicking on the hardwood floor, Benny slowly appeared.

"Apparently, his curiosity got the best of him, and he thought maybe he'd better check things out," Sweeny chuckled as Benny did just that. He stopped at Anne's chair and looked her in the eyes. Upon getting the desired attention he wanted, he did the same with Sally and also got his desired results. He just looked at Sweeny and returned to Sally for a little ear scratching and head petting and then flopped down by the fire.

Sweeny casually commented that he didn't have that newfangled gadget called TV as he felt he didn't have time to sit in a chair and watch it. As they did a second house tour, Sally commented that she found the kitchen delightful. She told Anne and Sweeney she wasn't the most diverse cook but could handle the basics pretty well.

Sweeney chuckled at that and said, "Maybe I could show you a few things, but you could probably show me a whole lot more."

The Sweeny house was built of logs and had extra insulation in the walls and ceiling. The front porch was wide and deep, as was the back porch. All the windows were extra-large, and the living room had an expansive front window. Sweeny explained that he liked to look out and enjoy the ever-changing scenery. They concluded the house tour in the larger bedroom.

He said, "Hopefully, you'll still be here after you give birth, and then you'll need the extra space. Benny and I will be down the hall. Let's save the tour of the barn and outbuildings for a warmer day. How about lunch?"

When Anne and Sally were alone for a moment, Anne said, "What do you think?"

Sally's smiling reply was, "A dream come true."

4

LEARNING RANCH LIFE

Sally moved in the next day after a shopping trip to town with Memory. Memory bought her warmer clothes, boots, and a down-filled parka.

"I'll pay you back," Sally told her.

"No need for that," Memory said. "Patsy gave me the money. She was beside herself with glee as she solved two major problems: finding you a place to work and live, plus finding someone to look after Sweeny. It's a situation that has been nagging Patsy to distraction for a while now."

Sweeny made a pot of beef stew for dinner the day Sally moved in. A big pile of it, so there were leftovers for the next day. He suggested they plan their meals once a week, so there was no confusion about who did what and when. Sally found this was a great relief to know what was expected of her.

Sweeny ran pretty much on schedule. He did the barn chores early, then came in for breakfast. Lunchtime varied, but he always told her what he would be doing and when he expected to return. If he went to town or some other place, he would always ask her to come along. She felt appreciated, something she had seldom felt, if ever, in her life.

Sweeny was not without some idiosyncrasies. He liked to get up at the crack of dawn and sit in his recliner with a cup of coffee. He would be found in his pajamas and bathrobe, sitting in front of the expansive living room picture window, staring at the dawn lighting up the scene before him. It was then he made his plans for the day.

He wasn't much of a drinker either but would share a beer or two on occasions with his friends. Shaving was another issue. He only shaved on Fridays, Sundays, and Wednesdays. He scheduled his appointments accordingly. He was a very happy man, however, as he did what he wanted. He felt that in life, ninety percent was good and ten percent not so good. So, if something falls in the ten percent not-so-good, put it there and leave it and enjoy the ninety percent good.

One day Sally watched Sweeny load up his old army surplus pick-up truck with four-wheel drive and chains on the wheels as he drove off and stopped at a gate, got out, drove through, stopped, got out again, closed the gate, and drove off. She thought about this for a moment and thought to suggest to him that she could drive the truck and save him a lot of time opening and closing gates. At lunch, she approached Sweeny about driving the truck. She said she was brought up driving stick shifts.

He laughed gleefully. "You're always thinking, aren't you, girl? You know, if you drive, once we are out on the feeding grounds, I can ride in the back of the truck and pitch out the hay without stopping, and that would be a real time saver."

Sweeny was always careful to collect all the hay bale strings, leaving none behind. He wrapped them around a post he had stuck in a stock rack holder in the back of his truck bed. If a string did accidentally fall to the ground, he would stop, hop out of the truck and retrieve it.

"I hate to see a cow or calf with one of those strings wrapped around their leg. Sometimes cutting off circulation and crippling them." At the end of each feeding, he'd throw the strings into a barrel for a trip to the county dump at a later date.

Sally drove on the feeding grounds where Sweeny directed and, therefore, seldom got stuck. Low spots were created at the gate crossing by the traffic at the wet spots, making a situation without a choice or opportunity to cross the gate opening in a dry spot. Sally just gunned it and, most of the time, made it, getting stuck only a couple of times. Sweeny would then take over and only once had to walk to the barn and get his old John Deere tractor.

Benny's habits changed also. On those cold rainy or snowy days, rather than following Sweeny around all day outside, he would take a walk around the yard first thing in the morning and quickly return and scratch on the door to be let in, spending most of the day laying by the fireplace. At feeding time for the cattle, however, he'd ride in the heated cab of the truck with Sally, seldom getting out.

5

BABY SHOWER

Spring was beginning to blossom. Trees and shrubs began to bud out, and tiny leaves appeared. Flowers poked up through the rapidly melting snow. Calves were starting to drop. And signs of the pastures coming alive appeared.

After feeding at the winter feed grounds in the morning, Sweeny saddled up one of his several horses and rode back to the same area. There, he checked all the cattle looking for any that might be sick or stuck with calving problems. Because they were still feeding on familiar ground, most of the cattle were there. However, a few seemed to prefer to calve on their own and hide somewhere further away. Somehow Sweeny could keep track of all these habits some cows had. Even if he saw a cow that was missing, he would look for her on his horse and do what might be needed, including pulling a calf.

Sweeny often came in late, tired, and dirty. He'd clean up and eat dinner, and he and Sally would then talk about the day. This kind of interaction was all new to Sally.

She had tried to write and call her now questionable fiancé with no results. The baby was getting bigger. She knew she would have to prepare for its arrival. So she began buying what she thought she'd need.

The girls at Patsy's place threw her a big baby shower one Thursday afternoon at the end of March, with Sally now in her sixth month. It was held at the Sweeny house and was a big event. Sally had known for some time now what Patsy's business was all about. Therefore, she was shocked to see several other women come to the party.

It was also true most were business acquaintances of Patsy, who owned several businesses in both Middletown and Riverton. It was also becoming apparent Ol' Man Sweeny seemed to be involved in several other mostly small companies also.

The guests all made it clear they felt good about her, particularly because of the fact that she was looking after Sweeny.

6

ROUNDUPS

Sweeny held his Spring roundup in late March or early April, depending on the weather. Fifteen or so cowboys and cowgirls would gather the stock, and they usually got them into the pens by noon. The ladies prepared a big lunch at noon, and by two, they all started sorting stock into what would be sold or turned back out. Then the rest would be branded, ear tagged, given shots, and the little bulls would get "fixed." Then they all were turned out, except the "sell" bunch.

Sweeny and his collection of good ol' boys would assemble with their stock trailers on Thursday to haul the "sell" cattle to the stockyards. A big dinner was served that night, with Sally amazed at how coordinated the women were. Quickly, however, she found out how all this happened. For the next month, every weekend, there was a roundup at different ranches. During the week, smaller outfits had a gathering of sorts. Wouldn't you know Sweeny, in his low-key unassuming way, coordinated all this for what appeared to Sally for years?

Sally attended these roundups at first with Sweeny's invitation and soon with the other wives' insistence. She had improved her cooking skills through Sweeny, and the ranch girls enthusiastically welcomed her presence. She really enjoyed life now, sitting on the front porch in the evening after dinner, watching the birds fly about, ending their day.

She liked hearing Sweeny commenting about the day's activities and plans for tomorrow. An owl hooted and flew about. Sally was captured by this quality of life.

7

LUKE ARRIVES

Springtime had now passed, and Sally just grew bigger with the child. Patsy's girls came around more frequently and seemed happy to do anything around the house to help Sally and Sweeny out. On that midafternoon June day, while Sally and Kat, one of Patsy's girls who came over every so often, sat on the ranch house front porch, Sally remarked, "I sure feel strange." And a moment later, her water broke.

Kat hustled her into the house and to bed. She immediately called Patsy, who dispatched Violet, who, among other things, was an experienced midwife, to the ranch. By the time Sweeny came to the house for dinner, it was all over. A healthy boy had been born, and the girls named him "Lucky" Luke.

Luke did all the things newborns do. He kicked his feet, squeezed his hands and looked about at this strange world, and cried for food or a diaper change. As the summer wore on, he progressed. One day he rolled over and was surprised at how different things looked, so he did it again. This was followed up by sitting up and frequently tipping over. He just hadn't figured out this keep-your-balance thing yet.

This was followed by crawling, and he began getting into everything. Sally was beside herself with all this extra work. He explored the contents of the lower cabinets in the kitchen and dragged things he found in them out to the floor. Sally then began tripping over the mess, chalking all of this up as a short-lived event.

Sweeny took it upon himself to install cabinet door locks. Luke was upset that he couldn't open the cabinets as this was where his treasures were kept, but he soon advanced to other things like opening the front or back door. As time wore on, Luke started walking, followed by running. Now, he was into everything, including Benny's food bowl and water. Benny took all of this in stride and, when it became too much, scratched at the door to be let out. Luke caught onto this and scratched on the door to be let out, but the door didn't open.

Ol' Man Sweeny made him toy trucks and cars out of two-by-fours, using sewing machine spools cut in half for wheels. He even went so far as to paint them in detail.

When "Lucky Luke," as the girls now called him, began walking, Sweeny began taking Luke with him in his truck while doing chores around the ranch.

He explained everything he was doing and why. How much did Luke understand at this young age is anybody's guess, but as time passed, Luke soaked it all up. Sally did well with all of this and welcomed the times when Sweeny took Luke with him.

She did wonder about her fiancé, Captain Tom Warfield. One day she would have to go to Camp Wood, Wyoming, to see him. She had written to the camp Commander, and he had responded by acknowledging that Captain Warfield was working there. He was doing well but seemed to have some communication issues. So, her visit was pretty much up in the air at this time.

8

LUKE'S FIRST YEARS

When Luke was two and a half, he began to babble incessantly. By the time he was four, he was a real talker. He and Sweeny talked at the dinner table and on the front porch at night. Sally was surprised that Luke understood so much about the workings of a ranch at such a young age.

When Luke was five, he and Sweeny made a trip to town. Luke hadn't been to town for a couple of years. He had never imagined there were so many other people, cars, buildings, and traffic. Then he saw something that really startled him, another child.

He never knew or thought there might be other children like himself. Luke was awestruck and couldn't wait to get home and tell his mother. After hearing her son describe his findings, Sally realized she was going to have to deal with her future. A trip to Camp Wood, Wyoming, was the first thing. She decided to go by herself. She talked to Patsy about leaving Luke behind and having the girls take turns looking after him and Sweeny. The girls were enthusiastic about looking after things. Sally had saved enough money to cover the trip expenses and then some.

She explained to Luke about his father and her need to see him. He really didn't understand all about of this, but he was okay with his mother being gone for a few days.

June first was set for her departure, and on June fifth, she would return. About this time, Sweeny had bought Luke a small lariat. Soon, with Sweeny's help and instruction, Luke began to rope everything in sight; cats, dogs, small calves, and especially chickens. Sweeny drew the line on roping horses and cows, but on occasion, Sweeny found Luke's rope on a horse or a cow that Luke couldn't get off. Sweeny chastised him, saying, "A good cowboy never loses his rope."

9

VISIT TO CAMP WOOD

June first came around. **The steam engines run** by the Union Pacific Railroad and the Riverton station had been dismantled. A diesel locomotive now stopped at Middletown, the county seat. The much newer passenger cars were a treat, and as Sally boarded the train, she found the cars were half-filled, which made for a pleasant trip.

It was a nonstop trip to Denver, where Sally would get off and take a bus to the town near Camp Wood. She arrived at Camp Wood early in the afternoon the next day and was taken to the commanding officer's office. Having written to him earlier, she knew her fiancé was still there but that he wasn't in good health. Major Thomas was warm and cordial, emphasizing that this was a very small engineering post dealing with water drainage, roadwork, and erosion issues. He explained that they did have a guest house where she could stay while visiting and that Captain Warfield would be in later that afternoon. He, however, wanted to talk to her first before seeing him.

The major proceeded to tell her about Captain Warfield's arrival some five years earlier. He had been brought to his office by a corporal who had met the captain, by chance, on a train. Shortly after leaving Cleveland, Ohio, the corporal found the captain wandering about on the train looking confused and disoriented. He said he had noticed the captain's branch of service was Engineering by the emblem on his uniform. The corporal then asked about his destination, and the captain said he didn't know. More questions were asked, and he found that he didn't know where his luggage was either. The corporal found a porter who knew where the captain had been sitting, took them there and found his luggage. The corporal saw a folder with his orders and suddenly realized they were both headed to Camp Wood.

As they talked about their mutual destination, he noticed a very large bump on the captain's head, but the captain seemed unaware of it. He told the captain they were headed to the same place, and he would get them both there. With that, the captain relaxed and promptly fell asleep.

"When the corporal brought Tom Warfield to me, he explained about their chance meeting on the train and Captain Warfield's confused condition. My first impression was to send him to the Army hospital in Denver as he wasn't making any sense of a number of things. However, after seeing several projects and maps taped on my office walls, the captain completely grasped the situation and even knew where the locations were.

"I knew he had been briefed on the proposed work back east, but he changed somehow. Tom even pointed out several obscure problem areas. He became eager to visit a site and wanted to go the next morning. I did arrange this trip and sent along his newfound friend, Corporal Kelly, who seemed to have a settling effect on Tom. The next day as we debriefed them about their trip, I couldn't believe how much information he had collected. There were practical solutions to many of the problems. Uniquely, he stored all of this in his head, along with many complex mathematical problems. It took us two days to debrief him. Immediately after the debriefing, we sent him to the Denver Army hospital with no tangible diagnosis other than the bump on his head had caused some kind of brain damage. How he got the bump, nobody knows. Ever since he goes to the field and is a genius engineer."

That evening after dinner, Sally was at Major Thomas' office when Tom Warfield came to see her. He was accompanied by now Sergeant Kelly, previously the corpo-

ral who had helped him on the train. With needed help, Sergeant Kelly likely got him cleaned up and in a Class A uniform. Nonetheless, Sally's heart fell when she saw him. He was gaunt and had aged twenty years. When he spoke, it was almost childlike and very soft. At that, he spoke very few words at a time.

"Tom, this is Sally, an old friend of yours," the major said.

"I don't know any women," Tom replied.

"Well, she is the one who sent you all those letters."

"I don't get letters."

Sally asked, "How about your parents? How are they?"

"All gone."

"What do you like to do now, Tom?"

"I don't know," he said slowly.

Then she asked him, "What did you have for supper?"

"I don't know."

And so it went on for almost an hour. Later back in her room, her tears flowed nonstop.

Sergeant Kelly was asked to come in and take Tom to his room. Sally held Tom for a moment without a response. Afterward, Tom shuffled out.

The following day, a soldier was assigned to drive her to the train station. Tom Warfield was already gone for the day.

She had said her goodbyes to Major Thomas and made sure he had her address. She told him that if anything different happened to notify her. She expressed her sincere thanks and, with a heavy heart, left without telling Tom he had a son. She had, however, told Tom in her letters but now realized he probably never read them or comprehended what she wrote.

10

LUKE AND EARLY ROUNDUP

Patsy Monroe met Sally at the train station, and Sally poured out her emotions and disappointment to her. "You know, you have to realize where you're at now, and that is being surrounded by people who love and care about you and Luke," Monroe said. "And Sweeny feels that Luke is the son he never had. He even bought Luke a pony with a little saddle and everything. Don't tell them I told you, as Luke is just busting to show you. Luke calls the pony Annabelle. While you were gone, they rode everywhere together. So let's face it, your future is not a grim one, but a bright one."

Luke and Sweeny were beside themselves when Sally came home. First, Luke showed his mother how he could get on and off Annabelle by using a hay bale. Then showed her how he could easily ride the dead broke pony and have her go and do what he wanted.

Memory had been in charge of the household since Sally's absence. She prepared them a delicious dinner. It consisted of chicken kabobs with yellow, green, and red peppers, onions, and mushrooms. All this was marinated in a honey barbecue sauce. Salad and corn were side dishes, along with dinner rolls. She also baked a cake from scratch that was not only a big surprise but delicious. Memory said wistfully she was sorry to go back to Patsy's and wished she was in Sally's shoes.

In fact, Sally began to look at the bright side of things. She came out of the house regularly to do things around the ranch. More neighbors' ranch wives also stopped by. Sweeny fixed Sally up with a horse that was compatible with her experience. She rode with Luke and Sweeny on the pasture and fence-checking rounds.

Along the path of growing up, Lucky Luke Wilson was introduced to mutton busting. Sweeny took him to the local rodeos where mutton busting was offered to the younger ranch kids to get them used to riding the rough stock (steers or bulls). These kids would be put on a sheep, gripping its wool at its shoulder while lying flat on the sheep's back. The sheep would then be turned out in a small arena. There the sheep would usually run and jump a bit, and the young cowboys or girls would simply fall off. Luke took the fall in stride and usually wanted another try.

So it began. Luke got better and stayed on longer and eventually began riding calves.

Luke began first grade with confidence. The many adults in his life had taught him how to count by showing the practical side of numbers by counting cattle, hay bales, and such. He already knew the alphabet and many shorter words on sight. The school bus picked him up at their nearby ranch gate. On rainy or other bad weather days, Sweeny or Sally drove him up to the gate and waited with him for Lester Bunch, the bus driver, to pick him up. Lester was a bachelor who lived nearby, so Luke was his first stop.

First grade passed quickly, as did the second grade. He was now eight years old, lanky and blond, and very active in practically everything, including roping. Anything that moved was subject to getting caught: Benny, chickens, horses, calves, cats, and whatever else, including other children. Wisdom led him not to rope his mother, Sweeny, or one of the girls.

Luke surprised his teachers with what he knew, especially in Math. The afternoon school bus always got him home in time for evening chores, followed by supper and whatever homework he was assigned, after which Luke would spend the rest of the evening working with Sweeny on various unbroke horses. Sweeny believed in the gentle breaking process. It was not unusual for him to spend a week talking to a horse, then brushing it down, picking up his feet, and following with a saddling up. After that, each horse was ready for the next step. When he felt he had the horse's trust and confidence, he would then get on and ride. By then, the horse rarely bucked or became a problem.

Luke was allowed to do this 'get acquainted process' and, by age nine, began doing some of those first rides.

"Luke, got one here that's determined to buck," Sweeny said one night. "Let's get you on and see how this comes out." Sweeny eared the horse down, and Luke climbed on. Buck he did, and with every ounce of energy he had. Soon the horse quit and just ran a few laps, then stopped. Sweeny said, "Get off now, Luke, but be careful. And I mean really careful. He's likely to spook." Luke got both feet out of the stirrups and jumped off. The horse spooked as predicted, bucked around the pen, and stopped. Sweeny told Luke, "Get a lead rope and tie him to the log part of the fence. Unsaddle him and brush him down a bit. We'll try this again tomorrow."

And so it went for the next three nights. Luke stayed with Firecracker, as he named him, on all the rides. But all the time spent didn't seem to improve Firecracker's attitude. When Luke came home from school at the end of the week, Firecracker was gone. "Sold him to that rodeo school down the road," Sweeny offhandedly said. Later they found Firecracker bucked students off pretty regularly. Sweeny now realized he had more cowboy on his hands with Luke than he previously thought.

Luke turned ten and was tall enough to reach the pedals in the truck. Sweeny had him driving everywhere on the ranch, sometimes on the county roads to neighboring ranches. Luke basically lived a quiet life as far as the outside world was concerned. But to Luke, it was rich and full. He had a best friend at school, Moose Harrison.

Moose lived in town and scrapped with other kids a lot. He was two years older than Luke, who knew Moose struggled a lot as his home life left a lot to be desired. The school bullies left Luke alone and showed him respect for fear of being smacked in the head by Moose. He became a frequent visitor to the ranch. Sweeny took Moose under his wing and taught him how to rope and ride, along with taking care of cattle and horses. He enjoyed all of this, especially Sally's cooking, which had become close to gourmet level.

Sweeny now had about four hundred head of cows. With two young boys, he easily got everything done, even though they had to skip school on occasion. Moose's schoolwork did improve enormously to the extent that he actually enjoyed school.

11

RODEO

Sweeny was still green breaking horses and, with the extra help, began putting a little more finish on his training. So his reputation grew, and more customers came to have their horses broken. Moose and Luke started rodeoing, participating in junior rodeo at small local events.

Moose was beside himself, even with his meager winnings. It gave him something to give to his mother and a few dollars to spend on himself. The idea of saving enough money and buying a truck really spurred his desire to enter more rodeos. Fortunately, the local rough stock wasn't too rough, as they found out when participating in larger rodeos. Age requirements kept them competing in the junior category, and the money wasn't spectacular.

At one event, Moose won one hundred twenty-two dollars and Luke fifty-six. They felt they were big time, but Sweeny brought them down to the real world. "Ride the local places, where you pretty much know you'll likely win something, rather than the bigger, more competitive events where you'll be out of the money more often. So, we'll work on developing skills, okay?"

So it became a hectic year. Sweeny slowly began to reduce his herd size, so he and the boys had more time to work horses. Sally helped with the chores and drove the truck in the winter while one of the boys spread hay for the cattle. Then, in late Summer, Sally came down with something that left her feeling ill.

"Case of the creeping crud," she explained.

12

SALLY

Within a week, she could hardly get out of bed. Luke and Sweeny took over the kitchen and housekeeping chores. They did some of the cooking. Memory came and filled in some of the time. They were all really surprised when Moose cooked a beef stew and, a few days later, a pork roast and continued to stay at the ranch most of the time.

It was fall now. The trees were shedding their leaves; the air was crisp, mornings frosty. One morning Sally asked to have the bedroom recliner moved to the living room picture window.

"I want to look out at all this beauty again," she said. They moved her recliner closer to the window, and Sally lay there, gazing out, with tears running down her cheeks. Memory drove up and, upon seeing Sally, immediately called Patsy, who hot-footed it out to the ranch. She looked at Sally and questioned her about her condition.

Then not thinking twice, she said, "You're going to the hospital, and right now! So bundle up. We're going."

Sweeny and Luke carried Sally to Patsy's Buick, and Sweeny told Patsy he would follow in his truck but not to wait on him. Memory and the boys cleaned things up. The two boys played cards without enthusiasm. It was eleven o'clock that evening when Sweeny came home.

"They really don't know what's wrong with her," Sweeny explained. "Got a bunch of tests to run, and I couldn't do anything to help, so I came home. Should know more tomorrow. Patsy is staying with her."

The next morning Sweeny left early for the hospital, leaving the chores to the two boys. He returned midafternoon and reported that Sally had double pneumonia and her blood count was way off. Doctors felt she would stabilize enough by Monday and could come home.

Monday came and went. Sally was not released as she had developed heart conditions and low sodium problems. Luke drove himself to the hospital to visit his Mother, borrowing Memory's car on Tuesday after morning chores. Upon seeing her lying there, wan and unresponsive, he had the feeling this wasn't going to come out well. Sweeny came in a few minutes later and confirmed Luke's thoughts. They worked out a schedule of who would be at the ranch and who would be at the hospital.

Saturday, during Sweeny's watch, Sally passed away. Overcome with grief, he found a phone and called the ranch. Luke answered on the barn phone where he was working. Devastated, he quickly did the night chores. After he told Memory what had happened, he drove to the hospital.

He found a grieving, tearful Sweeny. "You guys are the only family I ever had," was all Sweeny could say as he broke down yet again.

13

REGROUPING

Patsy took charge of everything. She purchased a cemetery plot, bought a casket, had the local undertaker take charge, and got a minister to do a service at his church. The word got out, and Luke was amazed at the number of people who showed up. He was numb to the attention he received and really didn't know what to say. Neither did Sweeny, who hugged and shook hands with everybody, but the tears continued to flow.

When it was over, they went home to the ranch, followed by the mourners, only to find enough food on the table to easily feed everyone. Memory and Moose had done all the chores early and were all slicked up, helping now to serve the food. They all became more relaxed and visited with each other and finally left. Patsy and her three girls and Moose cleaned everything up.

Luke now realized that at twelve years old and in the seventh grade, he was without a mother, or a father, for that matter, and felt somewhat lost. He knew all of this cost something, so he asked Patsy, "Who pays for all of this expense, the funeral and all?"

"Well," she said, "it's all paid for by my special slush fund account, and the cost of all of this is just a drop in the bucket to that account."

14

NEW PLANS

Sweeny was inconsolable and just walked around the house. One day he finally went outside but just continued to walk around. Luke had to call Moose to come over and help do chores and catch up on a few other things. Patsy came over regularly and consoled Sweeny and Luke. Weighed down with sadness, the boys skipped a few days of school.

One morning as one of Patsy's girls cooked breakfast, Sweeny said to Luke, "After we eat, we need to go down to the barn and talk."

They did the routine chores, then sat down in the barn on a couple of hay bales.

Sweeny started, "Luke, for a kid of twelve years old, you did a mighty fine job of keeping everything going. It was a good move calling that Moose kid to come over and help you. I realized I wasn't holding my end of the bargain, and I have begun to re-evaluate the overall situation here. You and your mother were totally family to me, which I never had. I always felt that you were my son. So, one day, this ranch will be yours. I had a lawyer fella here in town draw up my will, giving it all to you and your mother. I'll have him redo the beneficiaries next week. There is another person involved who I feel will be a real resource for you. More on that later, however. I also want to cut the herd size down considerably. It will be a lot less work, and if we sell our bred Black Angus cows to some cow/calf camp operation, we'll do well.

"We've got about four hundred cows now, but I want to slowly reduce that number to a hundred cows. We'll sell those three hundred at twenty head or so at a time at the local sale barns. I know a few ranchers who may be interested in buying a larger group. We'll be able to make hay over the summer and sell it in the winter. Some outfits may even pick up a winter supply straight from the field. Likely, we'll sell more hay to the small acreage and horse people. It will make winter chores easier and fewer stock tanks to have to thaw out."

Sweeny put the word out and immediately sold twelve head at the local sales barn, bringing top dollar. Then two ranchers bought eighty-four heads, creating a need for a mini round-up. Sweeny was up to that task. The two ranchers brought their regular hands to the round-up, and Sweeny and Moose helped guide them to where the cattle were on the range. The weather had turned colder, and snow was in the air. Fresh hay scattered in the corrals was all that the stock needed to attract them into the corrals.

Sorting went quickly, followed by food served by Memory and Anne. The next day the good old boys showed up with several stock trailers and hauled the cows to their new home.

15

MOOSE AND HIS AIRPLANE

By mid-fall, the weather continued to hold. Moose was two years ahead of Luke in school but continued to do well, all things considered, with his background and home situation. With the chores lightening up, they skipped school more infrequently, bolstering their grades.

With the herd size cut down, a noticeable difference became apparent. They heated the stock tanks with wood-fired floating heaters. Some stock tanks weren't needed now, so less wood had to be cut to fire them. They got all of this 'get ready for winter work' done. Soon the weather changed with snow and freezing temperatures. Moose went out for basketball and did well. He and Luke had made a backboard with a hoop, which they hung in the barn alleyway.

Moose had started dating Betty, who was in his class at school. She shot hoops with them down in the barn that fall. When Memory was at the ranch, she would come down and play. She had played girls basketball in high school and was able to coach the other three on how to play better.

Late that spring, Moose came up with one of his own surprises. His uncle Bill had passed away down in Oklahoma and willed Moose his airplane. He apparently understood his nephew's desire to fly, and this fabric-covered Piper Cub would get him started. Unknown to Uncle Bill, Moose had started his required forty hours of training when he was fourteen with money earned from rodeoing and at the Double B Ranch. He had just recently soloed. At fifteen, he got his official pilot's license. He asked Luke to go with him to Oklahoma and fly the airplane back home. Luke could only say no because of ranch work.

Moose was undeterred and set out on a bus to Oklahoma to pick up his airplane. He called his Aunt Millie from the bus station, and she came and picked him up, insisting he have supper with her and spend the night. He was pretty excited and didn't sleep too well. Aunt Millie fixed him a big breakfast, after which she drove him to the airport, recalling many stories about Uncle Bill's flying experiences.

The airport manager took it upon himself to check the Piper Cub out from one end to the other and even flew it around the airstrip a few times. "She's ready to go!" he told them and then asked where his first stop was. Knowing his top speed was only seventy-five miles an hour and his range only one hundred fifty miles, he knew his refueling stops would be not too far apart. It appeared to be a five-hundred-mile trip with four stops, likely about an eight-hour trip. The weather was clear and balmy.

He kissed and hugged his Aunt Millie goodbye and was off to his new flying career. Moose stuck to his flight plan, even though he was ahead of schedule. He made all his planned stops and arrived at the Riverton airport on time.

He proudly showed his instructor his newly acquired airplane. Moose quickly called Luke and told him they should get to rodeos in this airplane to save time and gas money. They started doing this, but other rodeo folks, hearing that he had a plane, wanted a flight to different destinations and began to keep Moose busy flying his airplane around.

16

GIRLS

Luke still caught the school bus up by the front gate. Lester Bunch, their neighbor, still drove it. He was an old bachelor with little ambition other than driving the children on the school bus, picking them up at their homes, dropping them off at school, collecting them after school, and dropping them off at their homes. He was a very solitary man, who didn't talk too much and had an affection for the bottle.

On days when Luke skipped school, or if the weather was bad and he thought school might be closed, he'd call Mr. Bunch. First, to save him a trip back up the lane to pick Luke up, and also to find out if he was coming or not. This kept him from having to stand out in bad weather for a bus that may not be coming. Bunch's response was seldom more than a brief sentence. The bus carried ten to twelve students, mostly from remote and rural areas, and was without any kind of communication service, such as a two-way radio.

One girl, Nancy Beckworth, also in the seventh grade, began sitting with Luke as they shared homework and assignments. She came from a ranch near Luke's. She was aware of his success with horses, and one day she told him that she would like for him to come over and look at a horse she was having trouble with.

"How about Saturday morning?" she inquired.

Luke replied, "We should have chores done by ten, and I can come over after that."

It was a blustery Saturday with gray skies hinting at the approaching snow when Luke arrived. He knocked on the door of the house. Upon being invited in and introduced to Nancy's parents and her younger sister and brother, he felt a friendliness he didn't experience very often. They all seemed to know more about him than he expected. Her father knew ol' man Sweeny and spoke respectfully of him.

Mr. Beckworth said, "When you're done with that horse, come in and talk with me about what's going on at the Double B Ranch."

Nancy had bundled up to ward off the cold weather. She bounced into the living room with a "Let's go!"

Nancy's horse was in a box stall in the barn, as were

several other horses. Fortunately, her father had built a round pen inside the barn.

"Let's get a halter on him and take him to the round pen," Luke said.

"That might be a chore," Nancy responded.

"How so?"

"Try it."

"How did you get him to the round pen?" Luke asked her.

"I herded him."

"Oh."

With that, he and Nancy got into the stall with the horse, Thunder, closing the door slowly behind them. The horse backed into the furthest corner and nervously faced him, unsure what would happen next. They began talking quietly about school, other kids, homework, and horses. He told her that Thunder was insecure to a breaking point, and having no experience with Thunder, he would take today as a starting point.

After forty-five minutes, curiosity got the better of the horse, and he took a few tentative steps toward them. He sniffed Nancy's coat first, then stood there as the two continued talking. He then gave Luke the once over, and Luke put his hands on Thunder's neck and said to Nancy, "Let's go to the house; I'm getting cold."

As they walked to the house, Nancy said, "What do you think?"

"Good looking horse with a few issues. Just do what we did today over the next week. Don't rush things. By next Saturday, we'll halter him and walk him down to the round pen. We've got to work on building his trust in us. Someone has slapped him around, and we need to get his mind set past that."

"How did you end up with him anyway? "he asked.

"Saw an ad in the paper with a picture. The price was right, and he was gorgeous. He belonged to that Albright family over in New Castle. They said they were going out of the horse business, and he was the last horse they had. When I saw him, he was running in a large pasture.

"Just turned him out as I wasn't sure when you'd show up. He's a little hard to catch when first turned out. That's what Mr. Albright said. He'd added that he was coming out by Middletown on Tuesday and would deliver him since that was a seventy-mile drive one way. I said okay, and Dad paid him."

"Nancy, do you have Mr. Albright's phone number? I'd like to get a little more information on the horse. I'll have Sweeny call him. Maybe say he's interested in buying the horse."

Nancy's mother had hot chocolate set out for them. Luke looked at Nancy in a different way as they sat down. Without her overcoat, leggings, knit cap, and boots, he appreciated how she looked. She was about five feet four inches tall, slender, with blond hair and blue eyes.

Her hands were calloused, and she looked pleased and happy.

Luke knew he wanted to know her better.

Nancy's father then grilled Luke about what he thought about Thunder and humorously commented about what was happening at the Double B ranch.

They both had been looking out the front picture window noticing that a large quantity of snow had collected on the Double B's ranch truck. Luke commented that he better head for home.

Sweeny did call Mr. Albright's number, but the number was disconnected.

17

THUNDER

Luke and Nancy compared notes about Thunder's progress on the school bus, and then they began talking almost every night on the phone about the day's events. By Wednesday, she had haltered Thunder and, on Thursday, led him to the round pen. Luke told her not to do anything on Friday but to go into his stall and see if he would come up to her immediately. If he did, just rub his head and ears.

When they met on Saturday, she told Luke exactly what had happened and what progress she thought she had made.

He asked her if Thunder had ever been ridden, and she said she thought so. Luke caught Thunder and haltered him in the stall, then led him to the round pen, walked him around a couple of times using a lounge line, then loped him a few rounds, after which he walked him all around the barn and outside. The horse was skittish about being outside, but Luke calmed him down as they walked. Luke suggested if the weather held, he wanted Nancy to follow a schedule all next week.

The following Saturday, he got Thunder into the round pen but didn't tie him up. He picked up all his feet, sacked him out with a saddle blanket, and saddled him. He got on and walked him around the round pen about twenty times. He then got off, shortened the stirrups a bit, and told Nancy to get on. She did and rode two or three times in the round pen. He stopped her by saying, "We'll quit now while we are ahead."

"I can't believe this!" was her only comment, followed by a quick hug and lingering kiss on the lips.

It was the first time a girl had ever kissed Luke. He liked it. This was followed by Saturdays riding on the Beckworth ranch. She would ride Thunder, and Luke whatever horse her dad wanted some time on.

Spring came with rapidly melting snows, water rushing off hillsides, and grass turning green. Calving at the Double B had gone well with few losses. The end of the school year was suddenly upon them. In June, Luke had his birthday. He reflected on the loss of his mother some three years ago and felt well taken care of. As a young teenager, he'd filled out a lot, and ranch chores had built him muscles.

Sweeny had no trouble selling off the remaining cows, leaving the Double B Ranch with some one hundred mother cows and the spring calf crop, which had been very good. They were green breaking four to five horses a month and were now doing more finished work on horses that showed promise.

18

SPRING DANCE

When school let out in late spring, the school put on its annual "schools out" spring dance. Nancy and Luke took it for granted that they would go together. Luke told Nancy he had never danced before and certainly didn't know how. Giggling, she said she didn't know either.

Luke smiled and said, "I'll look into this, but no one would notice as they would be shuffling around too." Luke mentioned this to Patsy, who then dispatched Memory to the Double B Ranch. Memory had taken it upon herself to find out what kind of music would be played on dance night. On a Saturday night at the Double B, music played, and Memory showed Nancy and Luke three easy basic steps for various music and followed those with dance lessons on several nights that week.

Nancy and Luke enjoyed learning those steps and began improvising some of their own. Memory then took it upon herself to take Luke to Middletown and bought him a pair of dress pants, a necktie, a shirt, and new boots. Luke found out later that Sweeny had paid for it all. Sweeny then decided to wash and clean up his old truck. Luke was beside himself with all this attention and thought about it as he drove to Nancy's ranch on dance night. He felt how lucky he was, even after losing his mother a few years ago. Everyone was kind to him. He appreciated Nancy's acceptance of his situation and her closeness to him. His life revolved around cattle ranching, horse breaking, and a warm relationship with Nancy. It was all that he wanted in life.

Stopping at Nancy's house at the door, it sprang open before he could knock. Mr. Beckworth was at the door beaming, "You look great, son!" he remarked.

Nancy came down the stairs looking so different, all made up. Memory had ensured Luke got her a corsage, which he then presented to her. Nancy's mother and father were very impressed and speechless. They, of course, had no idea who Memory was, nor was she normally ever mentioned. They just assumed she was some sort of a full-time housekeeper, hired and working for Sweeny. Mr. Beckworth commented on whether or not

Luke had a driver's license, to which Luke replied, "No, it had expired."

That generated a laugh from all of them.

Her dad said, "I'll drive you if you want."

"No, I can handle it, but thanks," Luke said.

"Okay then. Drive carefully."

At the dance, the music started early. The girls were all prettied up. The boys were slicked up, awkward, and unsure of what to do next. Luke and Nancy hit the dance floor first and shuffled until several other couples joined them. They hit their newfound steps, with the others mimicking their movements. And so it went.

Slow music came on, giving the couples a breather. The guys and girls kept cutting in on them, wanting to try the better dancers and their fancy steps. When Luke and Nancy finally got back together again, they couldn't contain their laughter about having only a few dance lessons and dancing better than the others. At least, that's what they thought.

Eleven o'clock came, and it was over. Everyone had a great time, and Luke and Nancy were looked at in a different light. Luke came out with stronger self-confidence, which he really hadn't had before.

Nancy's parents and siblings were up and waiting when they got to her house, wanting to hear all about it. It took an hour to cover who danced with who, and they even demonstrated a few of the basic steps. Luke said he needed to go as Sunday was just another workday for him. Nancy walked him to the porch, hugged him, and kissed him several times. When they parted, they both said, "When is the next dance?" and laughed loudly.

Luke was surprised when he got home to find Sweeny and, who else other than Memory, waiting for him, eager to hear about his dance adventures. He covered this experience in about forty-five minutes, nearly falling asleep.

Sweeny then said, "Don't worry about chores tomorrow. Take Sunday off. I got you covered, and Memory will have a great breakfast for us."

They all went to bed shortly after.

19

FLYING TO RODEOS

Luke turned fourteen that summer. He rodeoed as much as he could along with Moose. They picked up their share of pocket money riding saddle broncs and barebacks. Sometimes, Moose would try riding bulls, but that turned out too difficult to make a ride and win anything.

Neither could rope well enough to venture into roping, even if they had a good roping horse. Although Sweeny said he could likely find one, the boys were somewhat turned off by the prospect of having the burden of hauling a horse around.

Other than baling hay, that was about it for that summer. The reduced herd size made a big difference.

Moose had gotten his regular pilot's license when he turned fifteen. Cowboys kept him busy flying to various rodeos on the weekends. And livestock buyers looked for his services during the week. He was now looking seriously at maybe getting an additional airplane or perhaps just a bigger one now that he was earning more money than he expected at his age. He was hopeful of getting Luke a license to fly, also. Luke wasn't too excited about that prospect and didn't want to miss any school. Moose did skip some school, but his girlfriend Betty helped him considerably, and he managed to keep his grades up.

20

THE STINSON

Moose and Luke had flown to a rodeo in North Platte, Nebraska. Moose was disappointed that he was unable to accommodate two other riders who wanted to fly with him.

The Piper Cub was just a two-seat airplane. After landing, he saw a plane parked in front of a hangar. It had a for sale sign on it. Moose checked it out and found it was an older model, Stinson, and it seated four people. He found the owner, Bob Newbury, and discussed buying the airplane, trading the Piper Cub in on it. They didn't come to any conclusions but agreed to meet the following week.

Newbury flew the Piper Cub and Moose, the Stinson on that occasion. They finally agreed on a price and would trade following a certified mechanic's inspection of both airplanes. Bob hesitated and wanted out when he discovered Moose was only sixteen. He was further baffled when he found Moose's partner was only fourteen and was financing the deal. The airport manager confirmed the two boys were for real. He also verified Moose's logged flying hours were real. Luke then wrote a check out to Bob Newbury from his rodeo account using his rodeo name.

Moose found even more cowboys wanting to be flown to rodeos and back. He became seriously busier than he thought he ever would be.

21

FRESHMAN CLASS PICNIC

Midsummer came with an invitation from one of their new classmates, a freshman. It was for Luke and Nancy to attend a midsummer cookout that would be at Donna Porter's house in Middletown.

Luke and Nancy eagerly accepted, as did some of their ranch friends. Most of the kids that were invited, however, were from affluent families in town or were considered part of the "in crowd." But all of them were first-year students. They showed up midafternoon on the appointed day. This time Luke borrowed Anne's new Pontiac to attend the festivities. Music was playing in the backyard, and several games had been set up. Two men in white jackets grilled thick pork chops, and several women fussed over the dishes. It appeared to Luke that about half the guests were adults, apparently parents of the teenagers. At a side table stood several various liquors, and the drinks flowed. Numerous people among the adults seemed to know him, however, and spoke to him and Nancy respectfully about dancing, school, cattle, the breaking of horses, and rodeo.

Donna Porter's father, who owned two local appliance dealerships and stores, engaged Luke in a detailed conversation, mostly about ranching in general. Later Nancy remarked, "What was that all about?"

"Seemed to me he was driving at something, and I was a little uncomfortable," Luke answered.

Dinner was great, and it was fun to visit with the kids coming to the new first-year class.

When he drove Nancy home, they both agreed they had had a great time and felt they might 'fit in.' As he dropped Nancy off at her house, her dad came out and howdied up Luke, "Get your driver's license renewed yet? With that slick new car, you wouldn't want to get a scratch on it without one", and he laughed uproariously at his joke.

Luke simply said smilingly, "I just borrowed it from somebody."

Summer came to an end. Sweeny felt they were in good shape for the oncoming winter with plenty of hay to feed the herd of now seventy head of bred Black Angus cows. The horse needs were ever changing. Sweeny had considerably less to do, but he supervised Luke, Moose, and Nancy, who showed up when she could, working cows and training horses.

Luke was somewhat intimidated by calls he started getting from Donna Porter. She sounded like she wanted him to ask her out for a date or at least ask her out to the Double B Ranch. Donna didn't seem to understand that he had little time to do anything socially. Luke was basically very shy around girls, all of them except Nancy, with whom he was not going to do anything to stress their relationship.

22

SWEENY

Summer was drawing to a close, and the start of school was just around the corner. Sweeny and Luke were hopeful for another cutting of hay.

"Nothing like a little extra feed in case winter lasts longer than you expect," he said.

But Sweeny began feeling poorly. Luke told him to take a few days off and rest up. He surprised everyone by doing just that, but it didn't help.

Luke called Patsy to say that Sweeny needed to see a doctor. With that, she sent Memory to take Sweeny there. The doctor checked his vitals and immediately had him admitted to the hospital. There, they ran tests and concluded he had congestive heart failure and lung cancer. They kept him in the hospital for several more days and sent him home with medicines and instructions, bed rest being the number one priority.

Memory volunteered to come out to the ranch and look after them. She even went so far as to ask if she could have Sally's old job as their housekeeper. She said she needed a change of lifestyle.

Nancy, by now, had figured all of this out. Her parents thought Memory was a housekeeper hired to replace Sally. They were, however, puzzled that when they called, Memory's voice sounded different, as Hope or Kat might have answered the phone when they were there instead of Memory. Luke explained that this was because of acute laryngitis on Memory's part.

Sweeny did well for a week or so. Then he lost his appetite and didn't make much sense on the rare occasions he did speak. Luke had set his recliner in front of the living room picture window where he could look out at the barn and feedlot with the rolling pasture hills in the background.

On a day in midafternoon, Luke stopped and sat down next to him. They both just sat there wordlessly. Then Sweeny, in a strong voice, said, "Luke, we sure did a great job on this ranch. Your help has meant so much to me, and you and your mother were a real inspiration to me. With you both, I had a family. I'm so proud of it all."

While gazing out the window on that fall day with the tree leaves turning red, gold, and brown and finally shaking loose from limbs and falling gently to the ground, Sweeny just slipped away.

Luke knew it but didn't do anything. He'd wait until Memory came home.

As soon as Memory arrived, Patsy was called. She warned them, "Don't do anything until I get there. There is more to this situation than you realize."

Patsy had the undertaker come to pick Sweeny up and had the coroner fill out all the necessary paperwork and issue a death certificate. Again, Patsy bought a casket and cemetery plot. Sweeny was buried early the next morning without ceremony, service, or headstone. Later that day, Patsy called for Luke to come to her house as soon as he could. Upon his arrival, Patsy invited him to the shaded back patio with coffee and rolls. There was a chill in the air. Being outside all the time, Luke hardly noticed.

Patsy did notice, however, and suggested going inside her office.

"It would be more private anyway," she explained. They retreated to her office, closing the doors. "Strange," Luke thought, as he rarely got invited to her ornate and lavishly decorated office packed with pictures of famous people, plaques, small statues, and numerous other items apparently collected over several years.

Before, they always talked business in the kitchen with all kinds of people coming and going.

"Luke," she said. "We need to keep what I'm going to tell you between us. We've got some time to process what all is going on and keep everything on track. First, Swee-ny regarded you as his son and left everything he had to you. Maybe, not exactly what you think. Second, Sweeny and I were business partners for many years, so now you and I are business partners. The problem is you are a minor for another four years. Third thing, we don't own the Double B ranch or even lease it. It belongs to your neighbor Louis Simmons. Sweeny made some bizarre arrangements with him years ago when Louis had fallen on bad times after an accident he had. How they both flourished in this arrangement, I never understood.

"All the cattle and horses belonged to Sweeny and now you. Somewhere along the line, we'll visit Mr. Simmons and see how we stand. For now, we'll just tell people Sweeny is sick, and you are just doing what he tells you. And for that matter, this house we're in now belongs to you. Just the house, mind you. And the business is mine. Everything else we own is shared fifty-fifty. The horses, cattle, and hay, along with your rodeo winnings, are all yours. We have several accounts we share, and most with blind ownership. Those blind accounts are where I've been banking money that Sweeny received from his ranch profits. These accounts are scattered about with no banking business done locally.

"We own seven houses and a half block of rented businesses in Riverton, a full block in Middletown, and three other businesses scattered around both towns. They are all rentals, which I manage.

"We also have three ranches which we wholly own. They are rented on an annual basis and managed by Sweeny through a rental company, so the ranch owners don't know who they are renting from. One ranch is the Woodstock; another is the Windmill. The one you really want to keep quiet about is your girlfriend, Nancy's father's ranch, which we own debt free.

"Sweeny kept the rents and leases as I did with our other properties at reasonable rates and have had little turnover, especially the ranches. I know Sweeny cut them some slack in the dry years or when cattle prices fell. Our new shared slush funds have about two and a half million dollars in them all combined. I'll get your name on them by next week, even though you are underage. We'll also leave Sweeny's name on the mail, but we'll have it forwarded to me. Anne, who has been my accountant for a while now, knows how and when to pay bills and which pot to pay them from.

"As you can see, being left to this great wealth and being underage leaves you vulnerable to many very unscrupulous people. Due to my situation and the business I'm in, I am unable to formally claim guardianship of you. One of these people is Harold Porter, the appliance dealer. He has made it clear he wants to adopt you if given the chance. Again, I would adopt you or gain guardianship in a heartbeat, but given my business, no judge would allow that. The same is for Anne and Memory. All of us will be on guard. I feel we should meet weekly for a while, and again, I'll remind you that all of our accounts have a business name that is untraceable."

Memory stayed on the ranch during this time, but when the weather turned colder in November, she abruptly left to go home back east. She left Luke a letter:

"I hate to do this, Luke. If people found out I was living out here with you, there would be all kinds of hell to pay. I'd probably go to jail for consorting with a minor, and they would shun you like a medieval witch. So it's best and the only way, and a tragic shame at that, but I must leave. I love being here with you on the ranch. I love taking care of you and Sweeny and hearing about your adventures of the day. I love you, Luke, and always will. PS. I'll write soon."

But she never did.

23

THE BUS ROUTE

One December day, after morning chores, Luke walked to the bus stop. Already cold and windy, sleet began to fall. He didn't wait long before realizing that Lester Bunch was not showing up. Luke knew Lester had a drinking problem and sometimes drove the bus when he was noticeably intoxicated.

He went home, called the school, and, yes, the school was open. With that, he drove the ranch truck to Lester's house and found the bus in the barn. He started it up, got the heater going, and entered the house through the unlocked back door. He found Lester passed out on the couch, drunk with a bottle in his hand. He left, got on the bus, and went to the next stop on the bus route. There, he found six-year-old Sarah crying.

"I'm wet and so cold. How come you're so late? I didn't know what to do. My parents had already left to go to work."

"You're okay now. I'll have you sit by the heater," Luke said. He then drove to the next stop and picked up Billy, who only asked, "What happened? Where's Mr. Bunch?"

"Well, this won't happen again, so don't talk to anybody about this."

Several stops were empty, and when he got to Nancy's lane, he found her heading for home. He tooted the horn, and she turned around and waved.

Once on the bus, she asked, "What's going on?" and then chuckled. "I know. Mr. Bunch drank more than he could handle."

"Right," was Luke's only answer.

Only half of the usual riders were on the bus when he stopped in front of the school. The riders got off and arrived a little late, but another bus pulled in behind Luke, and it was all going to be chalked up to bad weather. At the bus barn, the attendant didn't say a word other than, "I'll gas it up and clean it out. You driving it after school?"

"I guess," Luke answered. "I thought they'd call school off today for sure."

"Well, the superintendent has to get the required numbers of in-session days so as not to cancel spring break, like last year. See ya tonight."

His classes went well that day, and nobody said anything about him driving the bus. Luke left his last class early. He said he had to use the restroom. His teacher excused him and said quietly, "Next time, just get up and go to your bus," with a knowing look.

The bus barn attendant just told him it was ready to go. "Just take it easy. There are a lot of slick roads out there today."

With a few riders more than on the morning bus ride, he set out for the return route. He took the slick areas in stride, which became a normal ride.

At Nancy's drop off, she said, "Thanks. Call me tonight," in a subdued voice.

He parked the bus at Bunch's barn, got his own truck, and drove home, not bothering to check on Lester.

Night chores went quickly, as he had only seventy cows to feed. He was green breaking just two horses. He'd gotten in five rides on each horse out of the twenty rides he usually sought to do, but today was a real drain on his emotions, and he went to bed early after checking in with Anne, who usually answered the phone at Patsy's place.

Since he was by himself at the ranch, it was felt he should check in twice a day with Patsy.

Later in the night, he was awakened from a sound sleep by the ringing of his phone. It was Nancy.

She asked without hesitation, "What's with you and that Harold Porter?"

"What do you mean?"

"He cornered my dad in town today and asked all kinds of questions about you."

"About what?"

"Like how many cows you have. How is Sweeny doing? How were you running things by yourself."

"What did he tell him?"

"Basically nothing. Said Sweeny was fine and that he thought you had some hired help. Porter did say he had plans to adopt you as you didn't have any living relatives."

"How come and why?"

"Dad said he thinks Porter wants your money."

Luke was stunned to hear this and became completely deflated. The result was he didn't sleep at all that night, wondering what this was all about. After chores that night, Luke did go over to see Patsy. She only confirmed what Porter was up to. She advised him to keep a low profile and not be seen too much.

The following morning he drove to Bunch's place. Found the bus in the barn. He just started it up and went to pick up the kids.

He unloaded the kids at school and dropped the bus at the bus barn. After school, the school superintendent met him at the bus barn.

"You've been driving Lester Bunch's bus route?"

"Yeah."

"Where is he?"

"At home sick."

"Or maybe drunk."

"Well, maybe."

"You got a driver's license?"

"No."

"Why not?

"I'm only fourteen, but I drive all over the state, hauling horses, cattle, and hay. At the inspection stations, they never say anything."

"I'm stuck with a very bad situation," the superintendent said. "I have absolutely no one who can drive or is even available to take those kids home tonight or pick them up tomorrow, for that matter. I'll see Lester Bunch tonight, so you'll have to run the route until I can find a new driver. So let's pretend we didn't have this conversation and get that learner's permit the day you turn fifteen."

So the routine of bus driving continued for the rest of the year. He got his learner's permit in June when he turned fifteen. The bus driving restarted in his sophomore year. Bunch was still listed as the regular driver, and Luke was the substitute. Bunch continued to get paid, but the superintendent made sure Bunch paid most of it to Luke. He was never able to find a route driver due to the remoteness of the area.

One winter day started out abnormally cold, with skies heavily overcast, signaling snow. The temperature indicated rain, but the result was sleet, somewhat rare for this time of year. It started just after lunch. The superintendent let school out early. Luke got to his bus, where the attendant had already put chains on the rear wheels, and he collected his riders. It became a slow ride, dropping off riders as he went.

At Nancy's house, Luke asked her to stay on the bus as he dropped his last two riders. He said he didn't like what the weather was doing and was uncomfortable about these last two riders. At Johnny's place, lights were on at the house, and a car was in the drive. He waited until Johnny was safely in the house and proceeded on his route to Sarah's ranch house. It was a fair walk for a six-year-old in icy conditions to make it to the house, so he drove up the lane to the house.

There were no lights on or cars in the drive. Nancy took Sarah to the door, where they found it locked. Sarah knew where there was a door key hidden outside. She retrieved it, and she and Nancy went inside. Nobody was home, but the phone was ringing. Nancy answered, and it was Sarah's mother who was quite upset. She said she had heard the school was closed early and was concerned about her daughter being home alone as it was evident neither she nor her husband would be able to get home for a while yet. Nancy then said she and the bus driver would take Sarah to Nancy's house. She then gave Sarah's mother the Beckworth's phone number. It was late at night when Sarah's mother and father slid their way home and then to Nancy's house. Heartfelt thanks went to Nancy and the now absent Luke.

24

BRONC CHALLENGE RIDE

That spring, Luke had a few dry cows he didn't want. So he took them to the Middletown sales barn. Some local boys who hung around the barn doing a few miscellaneous chores here and there always acted like they knew everything about anything.

"Hey!" one of them called out. "We hear you're a bronc rider."

Luke just looked at them.

"Well, I'll tell you what," one of them continued. "We've got a mare named Daisy who sometimes kind of crow hops, and we'll bet you that you can't ride her for thirty seconds. Daisy doesn't get a crow hop off any faster than ten seconds. So, that would give her three hops to unload you. We've got forty bucks that says you can't ride her."

"Well, okay," Luke responded. "But let me see her first."

They found her in a stall in the barn. Luke recognized the mare as the one he and Sweeny had worked with a couple of years earlier. Without another word, he said he couldn't ride her today but would next Saturday. That would give them time to draw a betting crowd.

Luke said he wanted the sale barn owner to hold the money, be the timer and judge the ride. With that, the guy who thought he was Mr. Big Shot Rodeo Producer gave Luke a big, yellow-toothed grin.

Luke went to bed early that night, got up at midnight, drove to the sale barn, and found the night watchman asleep in the office. Then he sought out the mare, Daisy, and immediately got reacquainted and started his trust-building process. After two hours, he quit and left. He hadn't brought any riding equipment, not thinking he'd progress as much as he had.

He did the same process the next three nights, riding Daisy each night. Toward the end of the week, he rode Daisy around the stockyard and even in the large pen where the Saturday event was to be held.

Saturday came and did draw a fair crowd. One of Yellow Tooth's gang said he'd go down to the stall and get Daisy. Luke said no in no uncertain terms.

"Show me where she is, and I'll lead her back and saddle her myself."

"You'll need help," Yellow Tooth responded.

"Hopefully not," was all Luke could say.

They went to Daisy's pen.

"Watch out, she bites."

"Right," Luke responded.

Luke entered the pen, and Daisy cowered in the corner. He spoke to her softly. He gave her a moment to think and then slipped the halter on. She walked calmly with him to the arena.

"You want us to load her in the chute so you can saddle her?" Yellow Tooth asked.

"No. Just stay back and out of the way."

With that, he dropped the lead rope, took a brush, and cleaned her off. With the lead rope still loose and on the ground, he began saddling Daisy. The bettors started to rethink this event.

Luke stepped on easily, and Daisy just waited for the rider's next cue. Luke cued her to walk and hollered out to the judge to start his timer for thirty seconds. After getting about halfway around the arena, the sale barn owner cried out, "He made the ride! And it's official. Collect your bets."

Yellow Tooth came storming in. "No, he didn't. He didn't come out of a chute and didn't have a flank strap on the horse."

"Don't remember anything about that. You said all Luke had to do was ride the horse for thirty seconds, and he did."

Yellow Tooth yelled, "He must have drugged the horse."

"We'll have a vet check that at your expense, of course."

Luke noticed Nancy in the stands and called out, "Anybody out there in the stands wants to try out this locally-owned outlaw horse?"

With that, Nancy waved and came down from the stands.

While shortening the stirrups, Luke asked her a few questions as if he'd never met her before. He helped her on, and she did a half dozen rounds at a walk and trot, with the crowd cheering and applauding. He helped Nancy down and collected his prize money. Yellow Tooth and his followers were nowhere to be seen.

This demonstration boosted Luke's horse-breaking business considerably.

25

HAROLD REQUIRES HELP

Harold Porter began his adoption efforts in earnest that summer and now was looking for help. Harold had known a local judge, Jimmy Matthews, since grade school. His main argument for guardianship was that Luke was a fifteen-year-old kid unprepared to handle a four-hundred-head cow/calf operation without the money to handle the revenues. His reasoning was that he, Harold, was a very successful businessman with three appliance stores, currently looking to open a fourth store in Centerville just as soon as he could close on a prime piece of property with a fairly new building standing on it. The Centerville location was some miles away. With Luke's help, while teaching him all about business and finance, he could easily succeed.

Judge Jimmy Matthews looked at Harold and said, "I suspect you'll have your hand in his pocket, in view of the fact he has some four hundred head of cattle running around, so what's in it for me?".

"Well, how about ten percent of what we get."

"Harold, as financially knowledgeable as you say you are, you don't seem to have a grip on Luke's earning capacity. What about that bronc riding deal at the sale barn a couple of weeks ago? The sale barn owner, Clem, said he made over five hundred dollars. So, I agree; where is that money now? So, I propose thirty-three, and a third percent comes to me, the same amount to you, and the same amount for Luke's welfare. That's more than fair for all, and there may be more expenses than you think. Get settled up on that property in Centerville and have a serious talk with the kid. I'll check around and see what I can find out about Sweeny. I know the kid says Sweeny tells him what to do, how, and when. I'm just curious to see what his bank account says."

When Judge Jimmy Matthews' investigator, armed with a court order, began checking the Sweeny bank accounts, he was perplexed in finding absolutely nothing. Patsy heard about this right away and knew it wouldn't stop there. Matthews, Harold Porter, and now the Sheriff's Department couldn't find anything. Reports came to her about property tax records being looked at and, again, finding nothing. They even looked at the coroner's office and did find something for a change. Sweeny was dead, meaning Luke was out there on his own. But for some reason, they couldn't locate the ranch. The mail was delivered to a Post Office Box. Property tax records showed no ownership of any property. No area banks showed any accounts, and they still couldn't find the ranch.

26

MAKING HAY

he second cutting of hay was coming up. Luke calculated the timing as to when to start the cut, rake, and bale. He knew, through Patsy, what Porter was up to and came up with a plan to put in place after the second cutting of hay was made in early fall. He had sold all the remaining cattle he had. He now only had four horses in the place, and they were only there for training.

He'd talk to his neighbor, Louis Simmons, who actually owned the Double B Ranch. Luke had heard at length about this bizarre arrangement he had made with Sweeny, but he understood none of it. He made a hay deal with Mr. Simmons and told him he would transfer the Double B back over to him. He explained what Harold Porter, Judge Jimmy Matthews, and the local Sheriff were up to.

Moose and Luke mowed the hay on the appointed hay-making day, finishing the second day. He and Moose then raked it on Thursday, so it would be ready to bale on Saturday. Most of the bale pickup and stacking in the barn could be done in a day if he had a good crew. He got Moose, his girlfriend, Betty, and Nancy to volunteer to help. Nancy's girlfriend and two boys from school also agreed to come along with their girlfriends.

Luke had promised them a steak cookout with a little beer and wine, as no adults would be there. Also, a small amount of pay would be included. All of his crew were ranch-raised kids who could run every piece of equipment he had.

The weather held, and the cut, rake, and cure time got done easily by Friday. Saturday came, and his crew arrived early. The only thing different was the hay was to be stacked in Louis Simmons's barn. Nobody thought to ask why. Luke told them to use lavish amounts of sunscreen, as he didn't want his crew to look like a bunch of overdone french fries that night.

Luke had borrowed a bale pickup and stacker from a neighbor and used three of his crew to do that part of the work. Then he had two crew members haul the loaded wagon to the barn and unload the bales onto an elevator. Luke, Nancy, and her girlfriend did the stacking in the barn. The loft became hot and dusty, and Luke peeled off his shirt. Nancy and her girlfriend followed suit. Shortly afterward, the bras came off also.

At the end of three hours, they all rotated jobs. Then three hours later, they shifted jobs again. At the end of nine hours, they were, unbelievably, finished. Something to being organized, as Sweeny would likely have said. With sly looks, the crew headed for the big twenty-four-foot cement stock tank that was about four and a half feet deep; some with a few clothes on, some totally without any, jumped in. They were ready to wash the grit and grime, sweat, and hay off. They swished their clothes around in the water and then hung them on the windmill structure to dry.

Luke finished up at the stock tank and started to fix dinner with Nancy's help. He had trouble concentrating on fixing dinner and felt he needed a short break with Nancy. So he excused himself to go to the house. Nancy followed.

Dinner came off well, and the crew unplugged the liquid spirits and consumed them moderately. Luke built a campfire, and they all sat around it. Then Luke told them that Harold Porter was trying to adopt him. If he succeeded, there wouldn't be any more days like today in their future.

He added, "No one is to talk about where the ranch is or any details about cattle or horses. Just say you've never been to the ranch, don't know where it is, and tell all your friends and relatives to deny any knowledge of the ranch."

The sun fell behind the horizon, and the crew began to leave quietly. Nancy called home and told her mother she was going to spend the night at her girlfriend's house but instead stayed with Luke.

27

SEARCHING FOR HIS PAST

Word began circulating about Harold Porter's desire to adopt Luke. This was brought on by a court order from Judge Jimmy Matthews to have investigators search for Luke's bank accounts at all the local banks and in the surrounding areas.

Only one account was found. It contained two hundred thirteen dollars and thirty-eight cents and never had over five hundred twenty-five dollars and eighteen cents in it at any one time. It appeared this money came from the cash of hay sales and income from breaking horses. Checks couldn't be written to this account, and it seemed that Luke occasionally withdrew money for personal use.

A few days after an investigator made inquiries at the bank, the account was mysteriously closed. By whom, nobody seemed to know. No other accounts were ever found in either Luke's name or Sweeny's. There was a lot of discussion in town about what Porter and Judge Matthews were doing. The community became very close-mouthed about discussing anything about these two and were very upset with Harold, Matthews, and now the sheriff. Local people and the newspaper made their disgust with these three men clear.

The building in Centerville was up for sale, and Porter couldn't come up with enough money to buy it. Luke and Patsy discussed this, and they both concluded they would buy the building and rent it to Porter at the highest rental fee possible. Mr. Beckworth had been visited by Porter, who told him that he needed to talk to Luke right away and how he could find him or, better yet, when he did find him, take him to the Double B Ranch. Nancy's father said he had never been to the ranch and had never called him on the phone. Then Porter asked if Nancy could show him where the ranch was at.

Her father exploded, "You leave her out of this, and if I find you do not, you'll answer to my forty-five!" He lunged toward Porter with a strong swipe at his face and broke his nose. At that, Porter hightailed it off the Beckworth property.

Luke and Patsy did buy the Centerville property at a reasonable price by offering a cash sale. All this was done through one of their blind accounts, now in a company based in Denver. A property management company offered to rent the property to Porter, who truthfully said he couldn't afford that suggested rental rate. The management company then told Porter that a nationally known company also wanted to lease the property. So there was a bidding war; however, the unknown owners would prefer to rent to local people to keep things more dedicated to hometown folks. They negotiated a lower rental rate, but one that Patsy and Luke felt would still be difficult for Porter to maintain.

Another issue was that Judge Jimmy Matthews said Porter would have to talk this adoption over with Luke and possibly have him come into his office. However, Porter still couldn't find Luke. Luke spread the word around, again, for people not to talk about where he might be and, particularly, where the ranch was. Nobody knew he was riding the Nebraska Junior Rodeo circuit and using a borrowed name.

School started that September. Luke had turned fifteen and had his driver's learning permit. Judge Matthews cornered the school superintendent as he had heard about Luke's school bus driving. He told him that Luke's school bus driving days were over, and if he ever got behind the wheel of a school bus again, the superintendent's job would be history. He also gave the superintendent a court order to deliver to Luke at school that day. It stated that Luke Wilson was to appear in court the following Tuesday at ten a.m.

Not having a driver that night, the superintendent drove the bus himself. He ended up at Mr. Bunch's house with no way to get home. He found Bunch passed out on the kitchen floor, and the superintendent decided to drive the bus home himself. He did stop at most of the bus riders' homes to tell them the bus wouldn't be running for a while. Their kids would have to find alternate transportation. He went to his office, sat down at his desk, and thought about all of this. He was fifty-eight years old and eligible for retirement. With a corrupt local government, he'd had enough. So he typed his resignation letter, signed it, drove to the School Board Chairman's house, and gave it to him without explanation.

Luke received the court order through his teacher; however, he failed to appear in court. A few days passed. When the sheriff and three deputies appeared at school and entered his classroom, they stood him up at his desk, searched him, handcuffed him, and led him to an awaiting patrol car that took him to the courthouse.

The acting school superintendent let the school out for the day. Rumors flew, and the whole county was enraged. Pressure on the sheriff was intense on how he had handled getting Luke to the courtroom. What the public didn't know was the high-handed threat that the judge had imposed on the sheriff.

"If you don't get him into my courtroom by two, it will be your neck in the noose."

So, along with the demands of having his investigator chase down nonexistent bank accounts, property tax records, deeds and death certificates, and other demands, the sheriff became unnerved, particularly with the current public outcry of Luke's arrest. So Sheriff Rogers resigned, effective immediately, and then hastily left town to an unknown location.

The public sentiment was that if Sweeny was advising Luke from his sick bed, they were doing a very good job. So why was Porter so hot-to-trot about adopting Luke? Most likely, it was the 'hand in the pocket syndrome.'

Luke stood before Judge Matthews, defiant and thinking he knew what was coming. He was a sophomore and close to sixteen years old. Adoption was coming, as well as the destruction of his plans for the future.

At the courthouse, Judge Jimmy Matthews stated in a friendly tone, "Mr. Porter was to talk to you about this adoption issue, and I see he failed to do so. I'll do it for him. The court order is now set for this afternoon, and Mr. and Mrs. Porter will be your guardians. You are to obey them with trust and respect. You will partake in meals with them, abandon your current home, and move into theirs. Mr. Porter is a very savvy and experienced businessman who will guide you on your ranching business, helping you work on and manage the ranch. If you don't comply with these measures, I will sentence you to juvenile prison until you are eighteen and give Mr. Porter full responsibility to run the ranch as he sees fit in your absence. Do you understand?"

"Yes, sir, I do."

"One more thing. I want you at Porter's house tonight and in school tomorrow."

"I have a request," Luke said. "I've got horses to return to their owners, cattle to move to their winter pastures, and several hay deliveries to be made. The hired man we currently have can't do all this by himself. So, I need at least a week to fulfill my obligations."

"Well, since you're being upfront about this, I'll give you ten days. We don't want to give a bad impression to anyone about how we do things, now do we? I think you'll find this agreement is in your best interest. By the way, where is this ranch?"

"It's out east of town about seventeen miles and north on Star Road."

"Okay, Luke. I'll trust you to your word."

Luke just hadn't said which town.

28

LUKE'S PLAN

Luke made a list of things to do:

One: Get Moose to work full-time until all the projects are done.

Two: See Nate Bloom, the cattle buyer, to come out and buy all the cattle he had left —which didn't amount to very much— but just those they missed on the last roundup.

Three: Return the ranch to Louis Simmons.

Four: Get his permission to tear all the buildings down.

Five: Get Nancy's father and Moose to tear everything down and give him all the reusable lumber to rebuild on his ranch.

Six: Get Moose to dig a big hole with a bulldozer and burn any leftover evidence of buildings or whatever might be burnable.

Seven: Then, have Moose take a bulldozer and level everything out, seed it down, and make sure everything looked like nothing had ever been there.

Eight: Then, fence the ranch entrance off with old wire and shrubs so it looked like it had been there forever.

Luke consulted with Patsy and Anne on his plan. They both felt this wasn't the thing to do. But given how desperate Harold had become, maybe they could pull it off. Also, Judge Jimmy Matthews' compliance on this matter was a concern as it could affect Patsy's and Luke's other businesses.

Following the gossip, the small-town community was certainly up in arms and avoided Harold's appliance stores like the plague. Patsy felt Harold's business would collapse within a year. She also felt Judge Matthews had overstepped his boundaries and wouldn't likely continue in his tenure of office, or if he stayed in office, he would most likely be voted out next election.

As long as he couldn't find the ranch or bank accounts, Porter was doomed. According to Patsy's sources, Porter was now deep in debt, and his business revenues had dropped considerably.

That wasn't Porter's only problem. Judge Jimmy Matthews was angry that all the paperwork and expenses for all the investigations fell to him to pay, and Porter wasn't doing anything in the way of financial support. When the two met, Harold convinced Jimmy they were on the edge of a solution. Any business transactions would have to come through Porter, as Luke was now in his custody.

Jimmy agreed with approving investigations to search the county with acreages large enough to support four hundred head of cattle, but Harold would have to pay for an airplane to fly over these locations.

Porter decided to hire an airplane pilot to fly over the ranches he felt might be the Double B and perhaps find Luke hiding there. He went to the local airport and found the manager. He asked about a pilot to hire and told him what he was planning to do. A few were suggested, but due to the cost, they were too expensive, and their available time was very limited.

"Who else could you suggest?" Harold asked.

"Well, there is one fellow you might try. He is pretty young and in school but has more flying hours than some of the others. He is also pretty busy on the weekends. However, he'll skip school for a chance to fly," the airport manager explained.

Porter said, "If he can and is available at a reasonable rate, I'll take him."

"Speak of the devil! Here he comes now. Mr. Porter, meet Moose Harrison."

Moose began flying Harold Porter to various locations on the far eastern side of town. They both agreed the ranch must contain at least four thousand acres or more and would concentrate their search efforts on properties of that size or more. Slowly but surely, they eliminated properties of known ranches. Then came to realize Sweeny likely owned the ranch under another name. They did find several ranches that could fill the bill as likely locations. Harold Porter then drove out on his own to check them out. Unfortunately for him, he encountered hostility and stubbornness. Meanwhile, his appliance business suffered considerably, as did his bank account. He reluctantly abandoned this search.

Luke's friends agreed to start a low-key campaign to get people to say that they didn't know where the ranch was or anything about Luke's bareback bronc riding. With all the buildings and the house gone, it would be hard to find the ranch, even if someone gave it away. Patsy had moved all of their shared bank accounts to a Denver Company with blind account names.

Louis Simmons wasn't surprised about getting his ranch land back but was extremely pleased. He didn't think too much of Harold Porter and could easily see what he was up to. He wasn't too happy about the buildings being torn down, but Sweeny had built them himself over the years, as there were no buildings there when they made their agreement.

"You know," said the barrel-shaped rancher, "Sweeny was awfully good to me, and you have been too, Luke. I'll do anything and everything I can to help you out. Just stop by to visit a little more often."

Nancy's father was happy to get the lumber from the barn and house. "That will keep Moose and me out of mischief for a while," he surmised.

Luke got the cattle rounded up with Nancy, her father, Moose, and his girlfriend, Betty. They weighed the stock and loaded them up. Luke was paid a fair price, much to his satisfaction. Luke signed the check and passed it to Anne, who deposited it in the Denver bank. All the cattle were gone, followed by the return of all horses to their owners. Luke had been paid in cash, which he also gave to Anne. She deposited that to the bank in Denver as well.

The tear-down work was moving along swiftly, and when his ten days were almost up, Luke returned to school. After school, he walked to Porter's house. Harold's wife, Sylvia, was surprised to see him and, at first, was unsure of who he really was as she had never seen him before.

Her two daughters, seventeen-year-old Donna and fifteen-year-old Tanya, came home and greeted Luke by name, confirming to Sylvia he was the real thing.

"Don't you have ranch chores to do tonight?" Sylvia asked. "The girls could help you, as Harold won't be home until late."

"No, I've hired a couple of hands to cover chores, but thanks. By the way, I've got a rodeo I'm entered in this weekend, Friday, Saturday, and Sunday. It's over in Cloverdale, and I've paid all my entry fees. You don't happen to have a car or truck I could use to get over there, do you? My old truck on the ranch is kind of falling apart, and I really need to replace it."

"Well, you'll need to talk to Harold about this," replied Sylvia.

"I will, and under this new arrangement in my life, transportation is a number one priority. It's not like I can walk out the front door at the ranch and have all the ranch needs in front of me and no transportation to do it. Well, now is homework time. Call me when dinner's ready."

Sylvia thought, "he's already asking for a new truck, and I didn't like his 'call me for supper attitude.'"

29

LATE NIGHT PLANS

The next few days passed quietly, and Luke barely spoke to anyone except Nancy, whom he ate lunch with at school. She reported on Moose and her dad's progress on rebuilding the house and barn, which was going slowly. He had to skip school Friday to ride in the Cloverdale rodeo. He'd entered bareback riding and saddle bronc events. He was maturing considerably in his riding and had developed a mindset just to make the full eight-second ride.

Friday, Nancy drove him to the fairgrounds. He made his first two rides easily, winning first in the bareback finals and third in the saddle bronc finals. While driving back and forth to these various events, Nancy and Luke talked about their future. Nancy's parents had drawn the line on staying overnight at these rodeo events. Now, Luke decided to ride as a senior competitor and use a different name. Clint Foreman was his choice. He got a new contestant card with the new name, and Nancy vouched for him as she actually had a valid driver's license.

The up-and-coming weekend featured a rodeo in Omaha. Moose was now flying him to some of the more distant rodeos. He entered and easily won the bareback contest but didn't do well at all riding saddle broncs. Nancy's mother accompanied them to Omaha, and they spent a couple of nights there. Luke felt things were beginning to work out. He was keeping Harold from seeing the ranch, and Moose was burning and burying any signs of it. Luke was beginning to place higher in the standings and was picking up some halfway decent prize money. Not a get-rich plan, but under the circumstances, it was the best thing for him.

Harold was gone a lot, but when he was around, he wanted to see the ranch. Luke had been able to dodge this by using school, rodeo, or the weather as an excuse not to go to the ranch. Then when he came home on Sunday and flashed around five or six hundred dollars he had won, that caught their attention. Harold always asked him for the money, saying he would keep it safe. Luke said he needed to keep it for entry fees and, on occasion, rental vehicles to get to the rodeo as he now didn't have any transportation at all.

"Sure could use a new truck," was his only response, and only a small amount was shared of his prize money with Harold.

Harold really began to pressure Luke to take Donna out on a date, often suggesting places he could take her; bowling, rolling skating, and movies. Adding that if he was short on money or needed a car, he would find a way to furnish those.

He also knew that Luke was soft on Nancy. If he ever took her out on a date, he couldn't figure out how he did it. It seemed Luke never used the phone or left the house without telling them where he was going. Harold occasionally checked on these outings, and apparently, they were legitimate. Little did Harold know that since there were no cattle or horses to take care of or even hay to sell, Luke had plenty of time on his hands to do whatever he wanted.

Luke was finally conned into taking Donna to the Christmas play decoration party at school to prepare the stage for the next night. They both seemingly had a good time, but Donna was far more interested in a boy named Alex. While driving home that night, Donna confided in Luke about how she felt and that she knew what her father was up to. She, too, had to play along with this, but they could work together and get around some of these obstacles.

"How about tonight? After everyone is asleep, I'll slip into your room, and we'll talk about a problem coming up. It's the spring dance."

It was about midnight, and all was quiet in the Porters' house. Donna, her sister Tanya and Luke's bedrooms were all on the second floor, while Harold and Sylvia's bedroom was on the first floor on the opposite end of the house. They rarely ventured upstairs. Donna slipped into Luke's room and his bed. They covered themselves up under the blankets to muffle their voices.

Donna started by saying, "I've wanted to talk to you for some time. But it seems someone is always listening. And you have been very standoffish and unapproachable when we are alone. I know what my father is up to. Ultimately, he wants me to marry you. He knows you have a lot of money coming to you, as you will have to sell some of your cattle sooner or later. He wants access to that money to clear up his many debts and shore up his failing businesses.

"The way I see it is you're waiting to turn eighteen, and getting through the next couple of years is becoming more difficult. I'm waiting to turn eighteen also. Alex and I want to get married and move away from here. So, if you and I work together, we can make the next couple of years more bearable. We'll pretend that you and Alex are friends. He'll come over and visit with you, but really to see me. You and I will go as a couple to the spring prom dance. We'll leave the house and go and pick up Alex and then pick up Nancy like it's a double date. So, let's try it out by going out Saturday night to go roller skating.

"It's been hard to catch up with you, and I'm glad we've finally connected where we can talk about this whole mess. We'll have to do something. I'm going batty worrying about everything. I feel there is so much going on in your life that you are keeping to yourself, and I don't know what it all is. So, let's try this dating thing, okay? Let me sleep with you for a while so we can talk about this."

Luke was unsure of what all this was about. He feared Donna might be setting him up as her father had no success intruding into his business. He only felt he'd have to go along with her plan for now and was surprised in part that she knew something was up with her father.

They did the dating thing with success. However, when school was out, Harold insisted Luke work at one of his stores. Weekends were devoted to rodeo. Nancy went with him to the rodeos most of the time.

The summer went quickly. It began innocently enough one night when Donna's sister, Tanya, slipped into Luke's room just to talk, she said. They got under the covers to muffle their voices. He learned more about Harold's plans for him, which included tracing his rodeo earnings to a bank account and the amount of his earnings. Luke realized that Harold would discover he was using a different name at rodeos sooner or later.

Tanya visited Luke's room more often. And he feared they would get caught, but they didn't.

Luke's biggest excuse for being gone was going not only to rodeos but clinics and other events. At this time, he was becoming a pretty fair rider. He sometimes said he was going to some far-off places and hitching a ride with other contestants. Sometimes he would go; sometimes, he just stayed with Nancy at their ranch.

He still worked with Harold a couple of nights a week at the new Centerville appliance store, which Harold had just built and opened a few months ago. Being farther from Middletown and Riverton, the local customers were not unduly affected by the local politics of those two towns. Luke was a gifted salesman, and Harold was very pleased as it helped his failing business, and he became less intense on getting into Luke's bank accounts.

30

LUKE VISITS HIS FATHER

Luke had two things on his mind. Now and again, to convince local people not to disclose anything about him or details about the now nonexistent Double B Ranch. The other was to look into his father's situation. He wrote to the commanding officer at Camp Wood. His return message stated that Camp Wood was being closed and that his father's condition, Capitan Warfield, had worsened. He had been transferred to the army hospital in Denver, Colorado. Luke resolved to drive to Camp Wood, Wyoming, and see where his father had worked these past sixteen years. Then to go down to Denver and see him. He explained this plan to Harold, who said he could go. But he didn't have any money or a car to give him.

"That's okay," Luke said, "I'll just take the bus, and I've got a little prize money that I've got stashed away."

"When are you going?" Harold asked.

"Now," he said as Nancy drove up in a new red half-ton, four-wheel drive pickup truck.

"Is she going with you?" Harold asked.

"No, her parents would never allow anything like that."

He loaded up his few things for the trip and then left.

Donna told her mother, "I'll bet they'll never come back."

Luke dropped Nancy off at her house and said good-bye to her parents. He took off in the red pickup truck that was actually his in the first place and drove to Camp Wood, which was a day's drive. There, he was greeted by Major Knox, now the Commanding Officer at Camp Wood.

He said he was just the interim commander, as Camp Wood would be closed in a couple of months. Even though Captain Warfield had been gone for a couple of years and hadn't gotten to know him very well, he spoke highly of him. He showed Luke his father's spartan quarters, now abandoned and seemingly empty.

Luke tried to comprehend that this was the room and bed his father had slept in for many years. With sadness, he felt the years his father never had to get to know and love him and his mother.

"This is his duffle bag with things he couldn't take with him to the hospital. It's yours now."

"Many thanks. I'll go through it when I get home."

Going to Denver and to actually seeing his father for the first time was going to be the hard part. Major Knox had notified the hospital that Captain Warfield's son would be stopping by. So, upon Luke's arrival, they were expecting him and ushered him to his father's room. There, he found a slightly built, gray-haired man sitting in a recliner. His eyes seemed vacant, but his voice was strong. He seemed confused.

"Are we going out to the field today?" he asked.

"No, not today, as you have a visitor," he was told by the nurse.

"That's me," answered Luke.

"Who are you?"

"I'm your son."

"Well, that's a good one."

"I came to see you, Dad," said Luke.

"We've never met before, have we?" his dad asked in confusion.

"No, but do you remember my mother, Sally Wilson?"

"I remember a Sally from Cleveland, I think."

"That's her," Luke said.

"I've wondered whatever happened to her."

And so it went for almost two hours, just a few fragments of memory here and there, after which his father fell asleep. Luke was disheartened but satisfied that his father was well taken care of; he did have a little memory of the past, particularly of his mother, but there was nothing he could do. He left, leaving Nancy's phone number and address.

Back at home, Luke's biggest excuse for being absent on weekends was a rodeo, and he was proving himself to be a challenging rider. Not up there in the top standings, but consistently in the top ten. Some weekends, he'd say he was at some distant rodeo but didn't go any further than Nancy's place. Sometimes she would go with him, with her parent's reluctant approval.

Harold never got Luke to show him the ranch. Luke claimed he had two cowboys looking after things, but upon being questioned, he never explained how he paid them. And, again, he couldn't take Harold to the ranch as the road was snowed in or too muddy, or Luke had to ride someplace in a top ten rodeo contest.

Luke started another campaign with townspeople, friends, and classmates not to reveal anything about where he was or the locale of the ranch to Judge Jimmy Matthew, Harold Porter, the local sheriff, or any of their investigators.

Then, there was always school which he faithfully attended. He volunteered to fill in at any of Harold's appliance stores on any weekday he wanted. Harold also had his hands full trying to keep his business afloat when he was suddenly called to see Judge Jimmy Matthews.

After months of no results, Jimmy laid it on the line. "Harold, you've had plenty of time to take over that ranch and have produced nothing, absolutely nothing. You are an idiot; all you have got out of this so far is a good salesman who works for you for free. That's the *only* thing you got going. A lot of time and *my* money has been wasted. With your failing business, you couldn't even find a three thousand acres or more ranch to get yourself out of hock. You're a stumbling, fumbling, dumb cluck as stupid as a box of rocks.

"I've paid for this mess out of my own pocket. And no longer will I do so. So I'm out of this deal. I will bill you for half of my considerable expenses and accept my half of the cost as a lesson in stupidity. You're on your own now, Harold. Get out of here. Good-bye!"

31

BAD NEWS DAY

One bleak, gray January day, light snow fell as Harold's world crashed. He came home early, finding Sylvia at the kitchen sink washing dishes.

She simply said, "Your cowboy is gone."

"Whaaaat! Gone, where?"

"I don't know."

"You sure?"

"He skipped breakfast, took his backpack, said good-bye, and said, 'see ya tonight,' and left for school right on schedule. Something didn't seem right to me. Being curious, I called the school. The lady from school said he never showed up, so I went up and checked his room. All of his belongings are gone, and the room was neat as a pin."

Harold's mouth sagged open. He went to Luke's room. Any evidence that he had used it over these last many months was gone. It was as spartan as it was when he moved in.

From what Harold saw, he realized Luke couldn't have carried all his things away in his one backpack. He apparently had very skillfully planned to leave for a while now. Harold called the school, where they confirmed Luke's absence for the last several days, but this wasn't unusual, as he was absent somewhat frequently. He completed all his homework and earned a straight A grade point average. So nothing was said since the school was aware of his ranching responsibilities. Harold wondered how a sixteen-year-old boy could outsmart him and where he would go.

His next call was to Judge Jimmy Matthews, who took the call but hung up as soon as he heard Harold's voice. Harold called the acting sheriff, telling him his son, Luke, had disappeared. The sheriff quickly responded but just as quickly toned things down when he realized who was missing and who was on the other end of the line. He told Harold to come to his office in the morning to sign a missing person report and bring any recent picture he might have of Luke.

Harold made a first-thing-in-the-morning trip to school. There, he obtained several pictures of Luke. None of them really looked like the Luke of today, as he appeared much younger.

Harold entered the sheriff's office and was greeted by the sheriff, who asked, "What happened to your nose?"

"George Beckworth hit me,"

"Why?"

"He got upset when I wanted to ask his daughter, Nancy, where the ranch was."

"I can understand this, Harold, as your tact and diplomacy don't exist, and you really screwed things up with Luke. So now, what do you think? Do you feel he's hiding on the ranch? Why?"

"Where else could he go?"

"Let's face it; Luke knows a lot of people who could and would help. And where is this Sweeny character? Surely, by now, you know what his status is. He's been dead for two years. All of this stuff you have ignored in your own brilliant way. Why didn't you have this Nancy Beckworth subpoenaed to court to testify about the ranch's location?"

Harold just looked pained.

"How much money have you spent with the anticipation of using Luke's assets? Do you have any idea how much money this sixteen-year-old kid is worth?"

"Well," Harold replied. "He's got four hundred head of cows, and at today's prices, that'---."

"Stop! Have you ever seen this alleged herd, or have you seen or know anybody or had anyone with authority verify that there was even a ranch? I'll spend a little time on this. I suspect something will come out of this sooner or later, but not likely to your advantage. You have filed a missing person report, and my department will act accordingly."

As Harold filed the report, the deputy at the front desk said he would put out that missing person search immediately. They would check all the rail stations, bus stops, and airports. Also, they would check all the truck stops on the interstate within one hundred miles. They'd get someone to check why there was no notice of Sweeny's death. They'd also look for any bank accounts he might have throughout the state. They'd also check property tax rolls on any land from two thousand five hundred acres to the greatest number of acres in the state. Someone must own this property. They would get Nancy to appear in court.

He was told that he could hire a private investigator to question everyone within a thirty-mile radius of where Luke said the ranch was. But this would be at his own expense.

Harold knew he'd have to sell something to pay for all of the expenses of doing this. The locals had really turned against him. He was to meet the deputy again at the end of the week.

32

HAROLD'S CASH FLOW

The various investigations didn't turn up much of anything other than what they already knew. Sweeny had died some two years earlier. They now knew, however, the funeral was paid for in cash by persons unknown and assumed to be relatives. The undertaker had also passed away, so they were left with the question of who these relatives might be.

Luke had apparently been running things by himself and likely was selling off stock when the market was favorable. Profits from his hay sales and horse training were untraceable, as he was almost always paid in cash. Where all this money went, only Luke apparently knew. Since there was no trace of Luke leaving town, the authorities concluded he was hiding on his mysterious ranch.

Harold went to the county office of deeds and got copies of every plat of ranches over five hundred acres in the county. There weren't very many, so he decided to hire Moose again to fly over these properties. Moose was very receptive to flying Harold on his search efforts as he didn't want him to get very close to the actual ranch location. So he just flew where Harold told him, just as long as it was not anywhere close to the Double B actual location. He also held out a tidbit of information after they had been flying for a while, often when he was running low on gas and decided he needed to turn to the airfield before he ran out. He would simply suggest to Harold, "Oh, there's a likely ranch straight ahead of us and to the left. We'll fly over that next time we're out. It looks like a good prospect to me."

Harold would enthusiastically get him to fly out to that location a few days later. Harold had also heard rumors that the barn had the Double B Ranch painted on the roof. Sometimes, however, flying to a prospective location and seeing some Black Angus cattle in the corrals or grazing about on the pastures, he would ask Moose to fly extremely low, right over them, so he might catch a brand. Moose refused, however, as this would spook the cattle and raise the anger of local ranchers, who would then likely call the local board of aviation and have his license pulled for who knows how long.

Since he didn't have any money, Harold offered to give him a brand-new set of a washer and a dryer for a few days of flying time. When he was not out flying with Moose, he was going over plats, ownership records, and just about anything else, but at the end of the day, he always came up empty-handed.

33

ENLIGHTENMENT

When winter came to an end, Harold had to close two of his appliance stores and was hopelessly in debt. So one February day, Sylvia told Harold not to go to work. She had something to talk to him about. When the girls left for school, she sat him down.

"Harold, you rank at the top of stupid men," she said. "You convinced our daughter, Donna, to throw herself at Luke to gain his favor and perhaps even marry her. You could never find the ranch or bank accounts you so dearly wanted, and now you can't even find your cowboy. And to top that all off, you're broke. I mean, really broke. A sixteen-year-old kid outsmarted you at every crossroad, including the sheriff, the judge, but mostly you.

"Well, hold on now! That's not my fault. We'll work this out."

"Why, of course, you won't hear that you are a failure. Great thinking, Harold. Having their rooms together upstairs and at the other end of the house, you never checked what might be going on up there. That's because that's what you wanted, right?"

"No!" Harold said with anger as Sylvia interrupted him with, "Yesterday, the bank sent us a letter saying they were foreclosing on our house. You were too busy to realize we were losing our home. All because of your infatuation with this kid's money. How much money does Luke actually have? Tell me! Okay, okay, I'll settle for a guess."

Harold said, "At least three hundred thousand dollars."

"But, you don't know for sure. All you know is a small account containing two hundred dollars and a few odd dollars at the bank, likely coming from rodeo winnings. He closed that account the day after he found out people were bound to be checking and looking into his bank affairs. It seems to me he's got some help. I'm sure he closed that account right after you wanted him to hand over his rodeo winnings. So, here is where we are now. In this pile of papers is the foreclosure on the house. You had been notified of this early this year and did nothing.

"There is a court order in that pile of papers stating you must leave now and can return at noon on Saturday.

By then, the girls and I will have moved out. The store in Centerville will be awarded to me, lock, stock, and barrel. The one in Riverton is yours. Mine is being inventoried as we speak.

"The divorce papers are in there, also. Just go to the lawyer who drew all this up and sign them. I have paid him in full with some money the girls and I had. We ask nothing from you except for the Centerville store and inventory. No child support, no alimony, as you have nothing and will have nothing in the future.

"Now for my parting gift for you. Remember, Luke drove the school bus for a couple of years. Likely, he lived on that route. For a year, you've been looking for the ranch in the wrong place in an area some forty miles from where that location is. Guess that was too much for you to think about. And the supposed location was completely wrong. That so-called pilot you had flying you around, Moose Harrison, is Luke's best friend. He would never fly you over Luke's ranch. It would be a cold day in hell if he did. He wasn't helping you; he was keeping you from finding it. You should have caught on to this sooner, especially when you came up with nothing after searching for so long. You need to take your papers now and leave. You have to remember that there is an injunction that restricts you from contacting the girls or me. Just one call from me that you're not abiding by the court order and injunction, you're in jail."

Harold left in a completely enraged state of mind vowing to find Luke and do away with him for all his misdeeds and refusal to receive his skilled guidance in social and business affairs. He checked the glove box in his car and found his thirty-eight-caliber revolver. He found it still loaded and ready to go. In a moment of calm, he went to the lawyer's office. The lawyer was understanding and said, "The divorce didn't incur any support payments or other costs. You should be able to do this and get on your financial feet easily."

Harold thanked him, signed the appropriate papers, and drove to the school. There, he found the new superintendent in his office. Using controlled calm, Harold asked about Luke's bus driving, who he was replacing, and where the route ran.

The superintendent stopped him by saying, "If this is a legal matter, I can't discuss it."

"No, nothing like that. Just doing some research on kids riding buses to school in an article I'm writing."

"Well, okay. What do you want to know?"

"I want to drive the route and see what it looks like. Maybe talk to that former bus driver."

The superintendent agreed to this and, on a map, showed him the route and where Lester lived.

Harold was gleeful with this new information and realized Sylvia was probably right. His first stop was at Lester Bunch's house. Now, a dilapidated, run-down place in desperate need of paint and repair. There, he found Lester, a drunk and shabby man. He asked him about the bus driving experience.

Lester squinted his eyes and leaned forward to look at Harold more closely. "You're that Porter fellow, ain't ya?"

"Yes, I am."

"Well, we've been told not to talk to you in any uncertain terms. So I'm following their instructions."

"Who would tell you something like that?"

"For one, Luke. He even threatened me."

"How so?"

"You know, kids. They like to run their mouths. But tell you what, for a bottle of Jack Daniels whiskey, I'll tell you what you want to know. And for two bottles, I'll even show you the ranch."

Porter then said, "Okay, I'll run to town and get some for you."

"May as well make those the half-gallon size," Bunch said, seeing this may be a windfall for him.

Harold hopped in his car and sped off. He couldn't contain his excitement at this enormous opportunity to solve his problems. He, having no money, went to his appliance store in Riverton, walked into the store, and went straight to the cash register. He opened it and, to the surprise of the store manager, who just looked at him, stunned to see Harold help himself to one hundred dollars and disappear quickly out the storefront door.

Harold drove to the nearest liquor store and made his purchases, quickly speeding back to Lester's place. He was giddy with excitement as he was so close to his quarry. He would catch Luke in his hiding place, and if Luke didn't comply with his demands, Harold would have Judge Jimmy lock him up. He would then do what he wanted, mostly cashing in any assets. He found Lester sitting on the front porch in a ragged lawn chair, looking expectantly for Harold's information gift. Harold gave him one bottle and said the other one was for when he was delivered to the ranch.

"I'll drive my car," Lester said, "and you follow."

It was only a few minutes to get to the ranch, which was Lester's first bus stop to pick up Luke. The road was now nearly invisible. It was now just a two-track that was almost never used and was overgrown with grass and weeds.

They stopped at where the gate was at one time.

"This can't be right," Lester exclaimed as he and Harold walked to where the now-absent gate used to be.

Harold said, "Where are the house, barns, and corrals?"

Lester said, "Looks like he tore everything down and abandoned the place. Likely sold all of this off to somebody."

Lester admitted he hadn't been back here for quite a while, maybe a couple of years, and didn't know what happened to the buildings, but this was Luke's place.

"The only traffic back here now looks like it's been just some kids to make out. Your Luke has fled the area. Maybe riding the national rodeo circuit, likely under a new name, but I doubt it. I've held up my end of the bargain. How about that other bottle?"

Harold passed it to him. He knew Luke had duped him again at an unbelievable level. Tearing down all those buildings was a major project done under everyone's noses. He stared out across the pastureland, now becoming green with rolling hills, backdropped with bright, pure blue skies. The horizon was filled with snowy white clouds. The contrast was amplified by the sun beating down. It was tranquil and peaceful.

Lester had driven away. Harold was devastated to realize Luke, a mere sixteen-year-old kid, had bested him in every respect. He also had lost everything he had ever worked for. He pulled out the thirty-eight-caliber revolver from his pocket, put it to his temple, and pulled the trigger.

A few days later, Lester sobered up and didn't remember seeing Harold's car leaving. He drove down to the old ranch entrance and found Harold's car and body. He called the sheriff and told him what had happened.

34

LUKE'S RESPONSE TO NANCY

Ayear later, Nancy Beckworth made a trip to Patsy's place and had her forward a letter she had written to Luke. She figured if anybody knew where he was, Patsy would know. The letter described Harold's misdeeds and difficulties, and suicide.

Ten or so days later, an answer came back via Patsy from a Sergeant Moose Harrison, U.S. Army, Vietnam.

> *'Good to hear from you. Sorry about all the things that have happened in my absence. I wish that I had been able to tell you when I was going to leave and how I did it. Basically, I borrowed Moose Harrison's birth certificate and had him fly me to Omaha, where I used the borrowed birth certificate to join the army. I needed to get past*

my real eighteen birthday, knowing what Harold was up to. I am sorry about Harold, but it was his own doing. Please forgive me first for my sudden departure. I'm so sorry I did this to you. Is there anyone living in the rebuilt house?'

Nancy responded with a letter full of details about what was going on around town. She had also talked to Donna and Tanya Porter and let them know Luke was okay but gave no details about where he was or when he might return.

Then, Nancy didn't hear from Luke for a month. Patsy called the ranch, saying she had a letter from Luke. Nancy hurried over and opened the letter in Patsy's presence.

'Nancy, I was wounded a couple of weeks ago, and I am recovering now. I'll be sent home soon as I can't physically be of any service to the army anymore. I would like to marry you and move into the old, rebuilt house that your dad restored. Only if your dad would approve, however, and, hopefully, with your acceptance of my marriage proposal.

All my love, Luke.'

ABOUT THE AUTHOR

Ron McCoy, has been writing and working with horses and cattle for over sixty years. He has participated in numerous roundups in Texas and Arizona. Trail riding has always been his favorite pastime along with writing. Illinois, Arkansas, Texas, Colorado, Kansas, Ohio, Indiana, Tennessee, Kentucky, and Arizona are some of the many places he's called home at one time or another.

Ron has served as Director and Board Chairman of The Indiana Trail Riders Association for several years. He has worked on ranches and boarding stables in his retirement years.

This is Ron's third book. He has two other books, *"Campfire Tales and Other Adventures"* and *"Murder at the Joshua Tree."* Ron has always felt that life is an adventure. You won't get it on a silver platter. You have to seek it out yourself.

www.ingramcontent.com/pod-product-compliance
Lightning Source LLC
Chambersburg PA
CBHW031251210726
48287CB00003B/987